Enid Blyton

Peter and the Magic Shadow

...and other stories

Bounty
BOOKS

Published in 2014 by Bounty Books,
a division of Octopus Publishing Group Ltd,
Endeavour House,
189 Shaftesbury Avenue,
London WC2H 8JY
www.octopusbooks.co.uk

An Hachette UK Company
www.hachette.co.uk
Enid Blyton ® Text copyright © 2014 Hodder & Stoughton Ltd.
Illustrations copyright © 2014 Octopus Publishing Group Ltd.
Layout copyright © 2014 Octopus Publishing Group Ltd.

Illustrated by Val Biro.

ISBN: 978-0-75372-658-7

A CIP catalogue record for this book is available from the
British Library.

Printed and bound in India by Manipal Technologies Ltd, Manipal

CONTENTS

CONTENTS

Peter and the Magic Shadow

Once upon a time there was a little boy called Peter who was very fond of sardines. One morning he had them for breakfast, and he ate seven sardines one after the other!

Now this is a lot for a little boy to eat, and his mother was quite cross with him.

"Peter, you really smell of sardines!" she said.

At that moment the cat walked in and purred loudly round Peter's chair.

"Look – there is Puss after you!" said Peter's mother. "Perhaps she thinks you are turning into a great big sardine because you have eaten so many!"

Peter shooed away the cat, picked up his school-bag, and went out into the sunny morning to go to school.

A dog came running up. He smelled sardines, too. And Peter had to shoo him away.

Then Peter set off down the lane to school. He took a short cut through the wood because he was late.

Before long a strange cat came running up to him. It was a brown cat with bright blue eyes and a very long tail. It smelled sardines!

"Shoo, cat, shoo!" said Peter. The cat ran away behind him, but it followed Peter all the same. It came nearer and nearer, and when Peter stopped in a nice patch of sunshine, the cat stood just at his heels, sniffing.

Now the cat couldn't eat Peter, of course, but as his shadow smelled of sardines, too, the cat began to lick up Peter's shadow! It licked and it licked, and very soon there was hardly any shadow left.

Peter suddenly looked down and saw the cat.

"Oh, you bad cat, you naughty cat!" cried poor Peter. "You're eating my shadow! Oh, I must have a shadow! Everyone has one. Whatever shall I do?"

He began to cry, and a little man came running from between the trees. He was a pixie, as Peter could very well see.

"Has my cat been hurting you?" asked the pixie.

"It's a very bad cat. It's eaten nearly all my shadow!" said poor Peter, sobbing.

Peter certainly looked very peculiar without a shadow. And the pixie was surprised.

"How dare you do such a thing!" he scolded his cat. "You greedy creature! Just because this little boy has eaten something you like, you nibble at his shadow! Why, there is hardly any of it left! Now what is he to do?"

"Miaow!" answered the cat in a mournful voice, very sad and sorry because it had done wrong.

"Can I buy a new shadow somewhere?" asked Peter.

"No, I'm afraid shadows are not sold anywhere," said the pixie, scratching his head and thinking hard. "I could cut you out a nice shadow from a bit of the night sky, of course – but it wouldn't really do for you."

"Well, you must think of something," said Peter. "After all, it was your cat that took my shadow."

"Oh yes, quite," said the pixie. He looked at his cat. "I know! My cat shall give you her shadow. She's eaten yours,

so it's only fair you should have hers!"

The pixie took out a pair of scissors and looked down at his cat. She had a nice blue-grey shadow stretching behind her. *Snip-snip-snip*! went the scissors, as the pixie cut round the shadow. When he had finished he rolled it up neatly and went over to Peter.

He took out a tube of glue and

squeezed some on to Peter's heels. Then he quickly stuck the shadow in place, and unrolled it till it lay flat.

"There!" he said happily. "You've got a nice new shadow! Aren't you pleased?"

Peter looked down, feeling very pleased indeed – but he wasn't pleased for long!

Poor Peter stood and stared at his shadow – for it was the shadow of a cat and not of a little boy! Wasn't that strange? There was the cat's head and pointed ears, four legs and a tail! Did you ever hear of such a peculiar thing!

"Take this shadow away! It won't do for me!" cried Peter. But the pixie was gone, carrying his cat under his arm.

Peter went to school crying bitterly.

He has got used to his funny little shadow now, of course. But if you know a boy called Peter, have a look at his shadow, will you? If it's just like a cat, you'll know how he got it!

The Village of
Untidy

There was once a small boy called Harry who hated to wash his hands or face. He didn't like brushing his hair, and as for cleaning his teeth, well, if he could possibly forget to, he would. He never had a clean handkerchief, and his shoes were always dirty.

"Dear me, Harry!" his mother would say. "Whatever am I to do with you? You look as if you've been up the chimney and then down again. You really are a very dirty, untidy little boy. Go and wash at once."

One day Harry's Aunt Sarah and Uncle Peter were coming to see him on his birthday. So his mother gave him a good wash herself, brushed his hair, gave him a clean handkerchief, stood over him

12

while he cleaned his teeth, and made him put clean clothes and shoes on.

"Now go and sit in the garden till I call you," she said.

So out Harry went. At first he sat down as good as gold, but soon he saw a very fat worm crawling out of a hole. Down he went on his hands and knees. The worm wriggled back in a hurry. Then Harry saw something moving down by the little stream that ran through his garden. Off he went, wiping his dirty hands down his clean shorts.

There was a big fish just underneath the bank of the stream, and Harry tried to get it. His shoes sank into the mud. He got his hands covered with mud too, and he wiped some off on to his face, for he was getting rather hot. Then he heard his mother calling him! "Harry! Harry! Your uncle and aunt are here! Hurry up and say hello to them!"

Harry knew his uncle and aunt would bring a birthday present for him, so he scrambled up as fast as he could and ran indoors. When his mother saw him, she gave a cry of dismay.

"Harry! Whatever have you been doing? Oh, you are a dirty little boy! Didn't I tell you to keep yourself nice and clean?"

"Shall I kiss Auntie?" said Harry, seeing a big parcel under Aunt Sarah's arm.

"Certainly not!" said Aunt Sarah, moving away in a hurry. "I never kiss dirty boys."

"You are very naughty," said his mother, angrily. "I shall not let you have

the lovely present that Aunt Sarah has
brought you. Go away and don't come
back until you are clean again."

Harry ran out of the room in a temper.
So he wasn't to have his birthday
present, just because he had got himself
dirty again! What did it matter if he was
a bit dirty? Why was everyone so silly
about being clean? It was ever so much
easier to be dirty and untidy.

"I shan't get washed and changed,"
he said to himself. "I shall run away!
Then when they miss me, people will be
sorry."

15

He ran out into the garden and
through the gate at the bottom, into the
lane that led to the woods. He didn't stop
running till he was right in the middle of
the wood and was quite lost. Then he
stopped and looked round.

"Now I'm lost!" he said, almost crying.
"Oh, I wish I needn't go back to nasty,
clean, tidy people! I wish I could live in a
nice, dirty place where people didn't
bother about being tidy."

16

Just as he said that he heard a splashing noise, and he looked round. There was a clear stream nearby, and on it was a boat, the shape of a swan. In it was a dirty little man, with long, rough hair, dressed in a stained, ragged suit.

"Jump in," cried the little man. "I heard your wish, and as it's your birthday, and you wished when you were standing under a hundred-year-old oak-tree, your wish has come true! I will take you to the Village of Untidy."

Harry stared at the ugly little man, and suddenly felt that after all he didn't want to go. But the man jumped out and caught hold of him.

"You can't change your mind now," he said. "Your wish has got to come true, whether you like it or not."

With that he pushed Harry into the boat and rowed off down the stream. Harry said nothing, but presently he began to feel rather excited. This was an adventure! And really, it would be rather nice to stay in a place where people didn't mind about dirt and untidiness.

Soon the boat drew up at a landing-stage and the little man helped Harry out. Just nearby was a village – but what a funny one! The houses were all crooked and neglected. The windows and curtains were black with dirt, and the gardens full of weeds.

A host of little people came running out and surrounded Harry. He thought they looked rather horrid. They all had dirty faces and black hands, and their hair looked as if it hadn't been brushed

for years. Their clothes were dirty and torn, and their shoes hadn't been cleaned since they were first put on.

"Welcome! Welcome!" they cried, and they took hold of Harry and dragged him along with them. "You shall live with us, little boy, and we will never make you keep yourself clean or tidy. You shall do just what you like."

"That sounds fine," said Harry, as he thought of how nice it would be never to wash his hands or face or keep his clothes clean.

The little folk showed him all round their dirty little village. Harry thought it smelled rather nasty, but he didn't like to say so. The houses were very dark inside too, because the curtains and windows were so black.

"We don't have washing day here," said the little man who had brought him. "We don't bother to clean our shoes, so we don't need to spend our money on polish. Aren't your shoes nice and dirty, Harry?"

Harry looked down at them. They certainly were dirty. No wonder his mother had been so cross. Never mind, nobody would be cross with him here. He could do just what he liked.

"Lunch-time, lunch-time!" cried one of the little women, and she rang a bell. Everyone ran to a big house in the centre and crowded in at the door. There was a long table down the middle of the big room inside and Harry found a seat there, along with everyone else.

At home there was always a nice clean tablecloth on the table, and the plates, glasses and knives and forks were always spotlessly clean and shone brightly.

But here it was quite different. The tablecloth was so dirty that Harry wondered if black was its proper colour. All the plates were dirty too, and Harry didn't like the look of his at all. It hadn't been washed properly, and was all greasy. His glass hadn't been washed at all.

A tiny woman called Trips served out some soup. Harry ate his, but it wasn't very nice. Then came some meat and potatoes and cabbage, and they were all put on the same plate as the soup.

"Don't we have clean plates for the meat?" asked Harry in surprise. "I don't think I like having the same plate for everything."

"Don't be silly," said the man next to him. "We have pudding on the same plate too. You ought to be glad to be here, a dirty little boy like you. Why, nobody made you wash your hands or brush your hair before you sat down!"

Then came a rice pudding, but the dish in which it was cooked had been dirty, so the pudding looked horrid. Harry wouldn't have any at all, but he didn't say why.

"Now lunch is over," said the little man next to him. "Come on, let's get up. I say, I suppose you haven't got a safety pin to lend me, have you? My coat is torn down the back, and I want to pin it up."

"I'm very sorry, but I'm afraid I haven't," said Harry. "Why don't you get someone to mend it for you?"

"Ha ha!" laughed the little man. "You forget we belong to the Village of Untidy. Why, we never mend our clothes at all!

Let me tear your shirt for you, then you'll be just as ragged as we are!"

The little fellow took hold of Harry's shirt and tore a big hole in it. Harry was angry. It was the last one his mother had bought for him, and it really was a very nice one.

"You're not to do that," he said, and he gave the little man a push.

"He hit me, he hit me!" cried the little fellow, to everyone. "Punish him! He's too clean for us! He didn't want his shirt torn!"

The little folk closed round Harry, and pushed him towards a muddy pond in the middle of the village. Soon poor Harry was covered with mud from head to foot, and his new shirt was all in rags. His hair was covered with mud too and stood up in tufts all over his head. Oh, he was a dreadful sight!

"Now you ought to be pleased!" cried

Trips. "You are dirtier than any of us!"

Harry walked up the street again, trying to rub the mud out of his eyes. He was frightened and angry. He didn't like these dirty, rude little people at all. It was one thing to be dirty himself, but quite another to have to live with dirty people. Suddenly he came to a small girl, sitting crying on a doorstep, holding her cheek.

"What's the matter?" asked Harry, stopping.

"I've got toothache again," said the little girl, sobbing. "It's very bad."

"Why don't you get the doctor then?" asked Harry.

"Would he make it better?" asked the little girl.

"I should think so," said Harry. "When I've got a pain at home, the doctor always makes me better."

Some people nearby heard what he said, and came up to the little girl.

"There's Doctor Clever-As-Can-Be, who lives the other side of the wood," said Trips, the woman who had served out the lunch. "He's doctor to the King of Fairyland himself, so he ought to be good. Let's send a message to him. The brown rabbit can take it."

So the brown rabbit was fetched out of his hole and told to go and bring Doctor Clever-As-Can-Be. Off he went at a great pace.

Soon he was back again and beside him walked the doctor. Oh, what a big, twinkly man he was! He wore a top-hat and spectacles and carried a big bag. But when he looked round the Village of Untidy he frowned.

"What a dirty place!" he said. "I've never been here before, and I'm sure I don't want to come again! Where's the patient?"

"Here," said the little people, and they pushed the small girl forward. "She's got bad toothache, Doctor."

"Let's have a look," said Doctor Clever-As-Can-Be, and the little girl opened her mouth.

"Dear, dear, dear," said the doctor, in surprise. "What dreadful teeth you've got, little girl! No wonder you have toothache. They look as if they have never once been cleaned!"

"They haven't," said everyone together. "We don't clean our teeth! What's the use?"

The doctor looked quickly round, and then gravely shook his head.

"Well," he said, "you'll each of you have bad toothache, and will have to have your teeth out, that's all. What nasty teeth you have, everyone of you – except this little boy. His teeth are quite good!" He pulled Harry forward, and looked at him.

"If you weren't quite so dirty, you would be a nice, good-looking little fellow," he said. "Do you clean your teeth?"

"Yes," said Harry. "Mum makes me."

"Then you have a good mother," said the doctor. "You haven't a bad tooth in your head! Have you ever had toothache?"

"No, never," said Harry.

"Of course you haven't!" said the doctor. "But I wonder if anyone else here has never had toothache?"

Nobody answered, and everyone went red. The little folk were beginning to feel rather uncomfortable. The doctor looked so very clever, and his voice was so very sharp.

"I want to see round this place," said the doctor, suddenly. So he was taken round the village – and how he frowned!

"Disgusting!" he said. "Horrible! Very nasty indeed! You ought to be ashamed of yourselves! Do you ever wash?"

"Never!" said everyone, proudly.

"Well, you will from this very day!"

said the doctor in such a stern voice that everybody began to tremble. "If you don't begin to mend your ways at once, I shall tell the King of Fairyland and he will burn your village to the ground, and send you as servants to the cleanest people in his kingdom. I shall return in a week's time. If you have not made yourselves into decent people by that time, you will know what to expect!"

With that he stalked out of the village, and left everyone trembling. At once the little folk called a meeting and sat round in a ring to talk of what should be done.

"Please, before you start talking, will you let me go home?" said Harry. "I don't want to stay in this nasty, dirty place any longer. I'd rather be washed six times a day and brush my hair twenty times a morning than be in this smelly hole!"

"Oh, you would, would you!" cried Trips, in an angry voice. "Well, you'll just stay here then! You know better than any of us how to be clean and tidy, and you've just come from a nice home. You must stay and show us how to do what the doctor has commanded!"

"Yes, he must, he must!" cried everyone. "And if the doctor is pleased next week, Harry can go home – but if he's not, he will have to stay with us for the rest of his life!"

Poor Harry! It was no good begging and pleading. The little folk had made up their minds, and he had to stay. So he made the best of a bad job, and looked round to see what to begin on.

"Oh dear!" he said, as he saw the dirty hands and faces, the long, untidy hair

and the ragged clothes of the little people round him. "I don't know what to begin with. You're all so grubby. I know! We will all start by having baths! Go home, everyone, get hot water, put it into your baths, and then scrub yourselves from head to foot. Wash your hair too. Then put on your dressing-gowns and wash all the clothes you've taken off. That will take you till bedtime. Tomorrow morning I'll look at you and see if you are clean."

The little folk ran off.

"And don't forget to wash behind your ears!" shouted Harry, remembering what his mother so often said.

Soon, in every cottage, the little people were scrubbing and polishing themselves. Harry went with the little fellow who had brought him there in the boat, and he had a hot bath too, and you may be sure he remembered to wash behind his ears. Then he and his companion washed all their dirty clothes and hung them near the fire to dry. Then they popped into bed.

Next morning, what a difference there was! The little people lined up in front of Harry and he looked at them thoroughly. Two of them he sent away in disgrace to wash themselves again and three of them had to go and wash behind their ears. Some of them had managed to dirty their hands and faces already, and he was very cross.

"It's not enough to wash at night only," he said. "You must wash thoroughly in the mornings too. And whenever you see you have dirtied your hands you must go and get them clean again. Of course, you must wash before every meal as well."

The little folk groaned loudly. Harry was quite enjoying himself. It was fun to tell everyone to do what he had so often grumbled at doing himself.

"Now, I must see to your hair," he said. "It's dreadful. Is there a barber here?"

"No, but there is one living nearby," said Trips. She was sent to fetch him and all that morning he did nothing but cut the little folk's hair neatly. Then Harry set them to work washing their brushes, and made them all do brush drill, brushing their hair this way and that till it shone like silk.

"Brush your hair night and morning, and before every meal," he commanded. "Now what about cleaning your teeth?"

"But we haven't any toothbrushes," said someone.

"What a dreadful thing!" said Harry, with a frown. "No wonder all your teeth look black. Go and buy some at once, and get some tubes of toothpaste too."

Off went Trips to buy the brushes, and when she came back Harry showed everyone how to clean their teeth really well. "Don't forget to brush the backs as well as the fronts," he said. "And remember – twice a day at least!"

Then he wondered what to set the little folk to next. He decided that they should have a lesson in shoe cleaning, and very soon everyone was busy watching Harry as he cleaned his own shoes till they shone. He was very proud of them when he had done, for it was the first time he had ever cleaned them himself. He made up his mind not to dirty them, because they really looked so nice.

Soon all the little folk had brightly

shining shoes, and then Harry decided that they must mend their clothes or make new ones. He asked Trips to see to this, for he wasn't very good with a needle himself.

Trips chose three more women and ordered everyone to bring their torn clothes to be mended. Trips had almost forgotten how to sew but it soon came back to her, and she quite enjoyed sitting there in the sunshine, sewing on buttons and putting on patches.

"Tomorrow we'll start spring-cleaning the village!" said Harry. "This is rather fun. Don't you think so, everybody?"

"We do feel much nicer," said the little folk, "and we certainly look much nicer!"

"Now we'll all go to bed," said Harry. "We've done a good day's work, I think. I shall want to see you all tomorrow to see that you've washed and brushed."

The next day only one person had to be sent away to wash again, and Harry felt quite pleased with the little folk, they looked so spick and span.

"First of all, drag all your furniture out into the sunshine," he said. "Then bring out your carpets and beat them. Clean your windows, and wash the curtains. Polish the furniture, wash the

cushion covers and do anything else you can think of."

Harry felt proud of himself. He had often watched his mother turn out his bedroom, and he tried to remember all she did. He poked into every house to make sure that the little folk were doing everything properly – and didn't he scold if he found someone shirking!

The spring-cleaning took a very long time. It was four days before it was finished – but how different the little cottages looked! They shone in the sunshine, and smelled so sweet. The curtains were clean, the floors were spotless, and all the brass glittered. Some of the little folk had found pots of white paint and made their walls look as good as new.

"Tomorrow is the last day before the doctor comes," said Harry. "We will make the village streets tidy, weed the gardens, and make sure that we have got all our clothes mended. Then we shall be ready for Doctor Clever-As-Can-Be!"

What a sweeping there was the next day! All the little streets were swept and tidied, and the gardens were weeded. Even the children were set to work to pick up bits of rubbish, and it was all burned on a big bonfire. Really, the Village of Untidy was a pleasure to see.

"Now," said Harry, when it was all finished, and night was falling, "be sure to have hot baths before you go to bed. Clean your teeth and brush your hair. Tomorrow morning, put on your clean clothes and come and line up in front of me before the doctor comes, so that I can see if all of you are clean and neat."

Next morning there was a clean, tidy row of little folk in front of Harry, all smelling of soap. Their hair shone in the sun, their teeth sparkled when they smiled, their shoes were brightly polished, and no one had a hole in his stocking or a rent in his coat. Just as Harry finished looking at them, a carriage drove up the street, and out stepped, not only Doctor Clever-As-Can-Be, but also – who do you think? Why, the King of Fairyland himself!

How the little people cheered and clapped – and how astonished and pleased the doctor was when he saw the spotless village and the clean, tidy people! He really couldn't believe his eyes. He went into every cottage with the King, and they were delighted with all they saw.

"Who has done all this?" asked the doctor.

"Harry has, Harry has!" shouted everyone, and the little boy was pushed forward.

"Oh yes, I remember you," said the doctor. "But you don't look like one of these little folk. Where do you come from?"

Harry told him and then, blushing very red, he went on to tell the doctor and the King how he had come to the village.

"I do want to go back home again," he said. "My mother will have been so worried about me."

"Oh no, she won't," said the doctor, smiling. "If we take you straight back, she will hardly know you have been away.

A week among the little folk is only an hour in your world, you know. I don't expect anyone will have missed you. Jump into the carriage, and I'll take you to the bottom of your garden."

So Harry climbed into the carriage, said goodbye to the cheering little people, and drove off with the King and the doctor, feeling rather grand. It wasn't long before he arrived at the bottom of his garden. He got out, thanked the King very much for his kindness, and bade him and the doctor goodbye.

"Goodbye," they said. "And," said the King, taking Harry's hand in his, "don't forget all the things you have taught the little folk, Harry! We don't want to find you in their village again!"

Harry promised and the carriage drove off. The little boy ran into his garden and there he saw his mother, aunt, and uncle.

"It must have been only an hour!" he said in surprise, as he heard a clock strike twelve. "It seemed just like a whole week, though."

"Why, Harry, you have made yourself smart," said his mother, pleased. "You're a good boy."

"And you shall kiss me and have your present," said his aunt.

It was a lovely present, for inside the parcel was a splendid fortress with a drawbridge and a dungeon. Harry was so pleased.

"Come on Harry, we're having lunch early today," said his mother.

"Then I must go and wash and brush my hair," said Harry, and off he went. Wasn't his mother surprised! She thought he was just being good because it was his birthday – but she soon found that she was wrong, for Harry was quite a different boy!

He never forgot to clean his teeth, always washed before meals and brushed his hair well. He even told his father that he wanted to clean his own shoes, and he couldn't think what had happened to him.

"I think the fairies must have done something to you!" he said.

"Well, you're right!" said Harry – but he wouldn't say another word!

The
Vanishing Potatoes

Times were very bad in the Village of Tuppence. All the brownies went hungry, and they grew thin and pale. Bron, their chief, shared all his apples and pears and potatoes with the others, but when they were gone the brownies really didn't know where to turn for a meal.

Only one brownie was well off – and that was Leery, the old, ugly brownie who lived by himself in a tiny cottage just outside the village. He had hundreds of potatoes, and was never hungry, for he could always bake two or three for himself whenever he wanted to.

"Ho!" he often thought to himself. "Bron may be king, but I am better off than he is! I shan't share my potatoes!"

Now Leery kept his potatoes in a shed

outside, and one day he saw a small brownie peeping through a crack at the piles of potatoes. He chased him off angrily, and then became afraid for his store.

"Suppose someone comes and steals my potatoes!" he thought. "That would never do! I don't trust these brownies. I think I shall bring all my potatoes into my cottage – then they will be under my eye and no one can steal any!"

So the next morning the mean little brownie filled his barrow full of potatoes and wheeled them into his small kitchen. He tipped them out on the floor and then went back for another barrowload. He spent all morning doing this and, by the time it was midday, the shed was empty – and his kitchen was piled high with brown potatoes!

"Goodness!" said Leery, scratching his head as he looked round at the hundreds of potatoes. "There's not much room for anything now. I'd better take my chairs into the bedroom – and the table too."

So he carried all the chairs and the table into the bedroom. He only left himself a small stool to sit on by the fire. There he sat, looking at all his lovely potatoes, pleased to think that he had so many more than anyone else.

Now, when the brownies saw Leery wheeling his potatoes from the shed to his kitchen they were very cross.

"I suppose he is afraid we might go and take some!" grumbled Bron. "It would serve him right if we did! Mean old

47

thing, never offering anyone even a bad potato! He can't possibly eat all those himself. He ought to share them with us."

"Well, Bron, shall we go and ask him to share them?" said another brownie. "He might, you know."

"I'll go!" said Bron. And so off he went.

He knocked at Leery's door and Leery called "Come in!" Bron stepped inside – and how he stared to see all the floor covered and piled with brown potatoes, and Leery hunched up on a small stool!

"Good morning, Leery," he said. "I've come to ask you if you will share your hoard of potatoes with the village. You have too many to eat by yourself, and the others are very hungry."

"What are you thinking of?" cried Leery, in a temper. "Give my potatoes away? After spending so much time and trouble in growing them! Not I! You're a poor sort of king, Bron, it seems to me, to let the Village of Tuppence get into such a state – and, by the way, I think it was very foolish of you to share out all your

food with the others. What's the good of
being king unless you are much richer
than anyone else?"

"What's the good of being king unless
you can help your people when they are
in trouble?" said Bron indignantly. "My
people love me, and I am pleased to help
them. I suppose you think you'd make a
much better king yourself!"

"Well, of course I do," said Leery. "Look
at all my potatoes! I've hundreds more
than anyone! I am rich enough to be king
twice over! And I'm quite sure all the

brownies would much rather have me as their head than you!"

"I'm quite sure they wouldn't!" said Bron. "And I do think it's horrid of you, Leery, to wheel all your potatoes out of your shed, as if you were afraid somebody would steal them."

"Well, nobody can take them now," said Leery. "I'd like to see a brownie steal any from me! Ho ho! Nobody could. Anyone can come and try – but they're under my eyes now, and not a potato can go out of this room without my seeing it!"

Bron was disgusted with Leery. He went out of the cottage and banged the door. He told the other brownies all that Leery had said, and they were very angry.

"Oh, so he said that anybody could go and try to take his potatoes, did he!" said Skippetty, a sharp-eyed brownie, thoughtfully. "Well, let's all go, one by one, and take his potatoes! We'll play a nice little trick on the mean old thing!"

"How?" cried the brownies, crowding round the small Skippetty.

"Listen," said Skippetty. "We'll pretend

that we are thinking of making him our king – and we will all go to his cottage, one after another, and talk to him about it. I will paint each of you at the back with strong glue – and, as there is nowhere at all to sit down except on piles of potatoes, we will each sit down on them – and when we get up there will be a dozen potatoes sticking to us!"

"Yes, but Leery will be sure to see them when we turn to go out," said Bron.

"Oh no, he won't!" said Skippetty, grinning. "You have to walk out backwards when you go out from a king's presence, you know – so we will each

51

walk out backwards, and Leery won't see a single potato! He will be so pleased to think that we are being polite to him! Now, where's my pot of glue?"

In a few minutes twelve brownies were all painted at the back with strong glue. How they giggled and laughed! Skippetty said he would be the first one to go to visit Leery, and he set off right away. He knocked at the door – *blim-blam*!

"Come in," shouted Leery.

Skippetty went in – and how he stared at all those potatoes! "Good morning, Leery," he began politely. "I've come to say that I've heard from Bron that you would like to be king."

Leery beamed broadly all over his ugly face. "Yes," he said. "I'm richer than anybody now, you know."

"Do you mind if I sit down and talk about it?" asked Skippetty politely.

"Not at all," said Leery, waving his hand towards a pile of potatoes. "I've taken all the chairs into the bedroom. Sit down on the potatoes. It won't hurt them."

Skippetty sat down hard, hoping that some very big potatoes would stick to him. Then he began to talk to Leery, and flattered the silly brownie so much that Leery nearly fell off his stool in delight.

"Well, Leery, I really must go now," said Skippetty at last, getting up from the potatoes he had been sitting on. "Goodbye. As you are now so grand, and may be crowned king any day, I will walk out backwards from your presence to show you how much I respect you!"

Leery could hardly believe his ears! To think that cheeky little Skippetty should be so civil to him! It was wonderful!

"Yes, do walk out backwards," he said grandly. "I am glad to see you know your manners when you talk to a king."

So Skippetty solemnly stood up, and then began to walk carefully backwards. He slammed the door and went down the path. Just round the next corner all the other brownies were waiting for him – and how they laughed when they saw him! He turned round and they stared in delight at fourteen large potatoes sticking fast to his back and legs!

"Oooh, Skippetty, what a lovely lot of potatoes!" said the brownies, and they pulled them off to eat for their lunch. How they chuckled when they heard all that Skippetty had said to stupid, greedy old Leery!

That afternoon two more brownies, one after another, went to call on Leery. They spoke solemnly to him about being king, and he was more and more delighted. They sat on the piles of potatoes, feeling them sticking to them, and could hardly keep from giggling.

One brownie brought away twelve with him and the other, who was a bigger fellow, took sixteen! They all shouted with laughter when the two brownies told them how delighted Leery was when they walked backwards most politely as they left him. They thought that was really a great joke.

"He deserves to be tricked," said Skippetty. "He is the meanest fellow that ever lived!" Leery was so pleased and proud to find the brownies really seemed to be thinking of making him king, that at first he didn't notice his potatoes were going. But, after six brownies had visited him and talked to him, he suddenly thought that his potato piles seemed to be growing smaller and smaller.

"Strange!" said Leery, rubbing his chin in astonishment. "How is that, now? Surely those brownies are not taking potatoes away with them? I shall watch very carefully when the next one comes, and see that he does not put any in his pockets."

So when the next brownie came to call

on Leery he watched him very carefully. But he did not see one potato being taken, for the brownie kept his hands in front of him all the time and did not once put them into his pockets.

Yet when that little brownie had walked politely backwards out of the room there seemed fewer potatoes than ever. It really was very strange indeed.

Leery began to get worried. He looked hard at the next brownie all the time he was talking but, no, he could not see him even touch a potato with his hands! It was very peculiar.

Then Leery thought he would call a meeting of the brownies and tell them to make him king at once. Then he could set them all to watch for the thief, whoever he was, and stop him from stealing his potatoes. He could not think where they were going to! So he sent a message to them by the next brownie that called – and how everybody grinned.

"We'll all go," said Bron, who was enjoying the joke as much as anyone. "We'll all be painted with glue – and what a lot of potatoes Leery will miss when we've gone!"

So off they all went, and filed in at Leery's door. They sat down hard on the potatoes, and listened as Leery explained they should make him king at once.

"If we make you king, will you be kind and share your potatoes with us, just as Bron did?" asked Skippetty, his little dark eyes twinkling.

That was too much for Leery. "Certainly not!" he said angrily. "I'm not so foolish. I might give you one each, perhaps. Anyway, none of you look hungry or thin now – you have all got quite nice and fat again, I can't think why!"

"Well, I'm sorry, Leery," said Skippetty, getting up, "but I'm afraid we won't make you king just yet. You may have plenty of potatoes, but you've got very little else. A king wants a kind heart as well as piles of potatoes. Goodbye!"

He went out backwards, and so did all the others. Leery stared at them in rage. When the last one had gone he looked at his potatoes in a panic! There were hardly any left at all! Where ever in the wide world had they gone?

He rushed to the door to call back the brownies and tell them about the strange disappearance. He saw them all walking down the street, chattering and laughing merrily – and he looked at them in surprise. Whatever was the matter with their backs? They seemed to be covered with knobbly brown things!

And then Leery saw what the knobbly things were – potatoes, of course! In a flash he saw the trick that had been played on him, and he tore after the brownies in a terrible temper, shaking his fists and stamping his feet in rage.

"You wicked robbers!" he cried. "You mean, horrid things! You've stolen my potatoes, yes you have! I'll put you in prison!"

"You can't!" said the laughing brownies. "Bron is our king – and *he* wouldn't put us in prison, we are sure! Remember, Leery, you told him that anyone might take your potatoes if he could – and so we have! We have only obeyed you, that's all! If you hadn't been so vain, thinking you were going to be

king, you would have seen what we were doing!"

"Give my back my potatoes!" yelled Leery.

"We've eaten most of them," said Skippetty with a grin. "Don't worry, Leery – when better times come we will pay you for the ones we have taken. It serves you right to be tricked – you are too mean for anything!"

Back went Leery to his cottage, crying tears of rage all down his long nose – and would you believe it, when he got to his door there was not a single potato left in the kitchen! The rats had popped in and taken every last one while he had gone after the brownies!

So Leery had to go hungry too, and it did him a lot of good. He felt far too ashamed to face the brownies of Tuppence Village, so he packed and left. He turned over a new leaf and tried not to be mean – and I shouldn't be surprised to hear that he becomes a king one day. But I'm quite sure he won't let anyone walk out backwards when they take leave of him. Aren't you?

The Goose that
Made a Hurricane

Once upon a time there was a big grey goose. She had very large wings and when she stood on her toes and flapped them, she made quite a wind.

One day she went to a little hillock and, standing on the top, she flapped her wings very hard indeed. No sooner had she finished than a wind began to blow from the west. It almost blew the grey

goose off the hillock and she looked round her in surprise.

"Good gracious!" she said. "Look what a wind I've started! I only just flapped my wings a few times, and I have made this great wind! How powerful I am! I must go and tell Porker the pig."

So off she waddled. Soon she came to the sty where Porker the pig lived. Bits of straw were flying all about and Porker was standing with his back to the wind, for he did not like it.

"I've some news for you, Porker," said the grey goose. "Do you know, I just stood up on the little hillock and flapped my wings a few times, and that started this big wind blowing!"

"What a strange thing!" said Porker, staring at the grey goose with his little round eyes. "Shall we go and tell Gobble the turkey?"

"Yes, let's," said the goose proudly. So they went across the farmyard to where Gobble the turkey was sheltering from the wind which now had almost become a gale.

"We've some news for you, Gobble," said Porker the pig. "Do you know, the grey goose just stood up on the little hillock to flap her wings a few times, and that started this big wind blowing!"

"What a curious thing!" said Gobble, staring at the grey goose in surprise. "Shall we go and tell Neddy the donkey?"

"Yes, let's," said the grey goose and the pig. So they went across to the field where Neddy the donkey was standing beneath a tree, trying to get away from the great wind.

"We've some news for you, Neddy," said Gobble the turkey. "Do you know, the grey goose just stood up on the little hillock to flap her wings a few times, and that started this big wind blowing!"

"What a wonderful thing!" said Neddy, staring at the grey goose in astonishment. "Shall we go and tell Frisky the lamb?"

"Yes, let's," said the grey goose, the pig and the turkey. So they hurried to the other end of the field where Frisky the lamb stood by himself, very much frightened of the big wind that was almost blowing his long tail off.

"We've some news for you, Frisky," said Neddy the donkey. "Do you know, the grey goose just stood up on the little hillock to flap her wings a few times, and that started this big wind blowing!"

"What a funny thing!" said Frisky, staring at the grey goose with startled eyes. "Shall we go and tell Trotter the horse?"

"Yes, let's," said the grey goose, the pig, the turkey, and the donkey. So they hurried to the farmyard and went to the shed where Trotter stood, listening to the big gale that blew all round.

"We've some news for you, Trotter," said Frisky the lamb. "Do you know, the

grey goose just stood up on the little hillock to flap her wings a few times, and that started this big wind blowing!"

"What a marvellous thing!" said old Trotter the horse. "If she can do things like that, you had better make her queen of the farmyard!"

So they made the grey goose queen, and she was very proud indeed.

The wind went on blowing and blowing. It got stronger and stronger, it became a gale, and then it turned into a hurricane and blew roofs and tiles and chimneys off! Everyone was frightened, and all the farmyard folk went to hide. Only the grey goose was pleased, for she was queen, and she was proud to think she had caused such a terrible gale.

After a time, Rover the yard dog came trotting into the yard, his ears blown flat back by the wind. He looked very cross indeed.

"What's the matter?" Porker asked.

"Quite enough!" growled Rover. "I was eating the finest, juiciest bone I'd had for months when this great gale blew up from nowhere and took my bone along with it!"

"Oh, this gale didn't spring up from nowhere," said Porker the pig. "Haven't you heard the news? We've made the grey goose queen of the farmyard because she was clever enough to start this hurricane by just flapping her wings a few times! Isn't she wonderful!"

"No, she isn't," said Rover, in a temper. "The horrid gale has blown away my bone. And what nonsense to say a goose could start a wind! Can she stop it, Porker, do you know? If she can start it, she can stop it, and perhaps I can find my bone again."

"Oh, I'm sure she can stop it," said the pig. "Come and ask her!"

So they went to ask the grey goose to stop the hurricane.

"It's your gale," said Rover, "so just stop it, grey goose, or I'll bite you. It's taken away my best bone."

The grey goose stood up on her toes, opened her beak and shouted "Stop!"

to the gale. But it didn't take any notice at all. It just went on blowing and roaring and racing.

"I don't believe you started this wind," said the dog. "You're only a stupid, ordinary goose, so how could you? You think too much of yourself, that's what it is! Hurry up and stop it or I'll bite you!"

"I *did* start the gale!" said the grey goose. "Look, I just stood up like this and opened out my wings like this – Oh! Oh! Oh!" And well might the poor grey goose cry "Oh, oh, oh!" for the wind took

hold of her big wings and lifted her right up into the air. Off she went with the gale, and all the farmyard stared in astonishment and wonder.

"That's what comes of meddling with winds and things like that," said Rover. "My advice to you all is to go to your sheds and hide there till this dreadful hurricane is over!"

Off they all went, hurry-scurry, the pig and the turkey, the donkey and the lamb, the horse and the dog. But as for the grey goose, no one has ever heard what became of her, for she was never seen again.

Mr Dozey's Dream

Mr Dozey lived just outside Tiptop Village in a dirty little tumbledown cottage. He was a fat and lazy fellow who never did a day's work if he could help it.

One day he had a very pleasant surprise. Mr and Mrs Tuck-In were giving a party, and they asked everyone in the village, even old Mr Dozey! The postman put his invitation through his letterbox, and he was most surprised when he opened it.

"A party! I haven't been to one for years," said Dozey. "The thing is, what am I to wear? I want a new coat and waistcoat and a new pair of trousers and a hat and pair of shoes. Can I borrow them from anyone?"

But nobody would lend old Dozey

anything. They had got tired of that
years ago. Whatever they lent Dozey
never came back!

Everyone said the same thing to him
when he came asking for clothes for the
party. "Dozey, you go and do what
everyone else does, you work a bit, and
earn some money to buy your own
clothes!"

Dozey was annoyed. "How mean they
are!" he said to Blinks, his cat. "Not a
scrap of kindness in them. Well, I've a
good mind to go along to old Ma Shuffle

and borrow a spell. If she'd give me a change-a-bit spell I could use it on my old clothes, and change them into new ones." This seemed a very good idea indeed to Dozey. He appeared at Ma's door, and smiled and bowed.

"What do you want?" said Ma briskly. "Come to ask for a job of work? Well, you go into my garden and do a bit of weeding, and you might sweep the path while you're about it, and there's a corner over there that wants digging, and..."

Dozey was horrified. What, do all that work! What was Ma thinking of?

"I came to borrow a change-a-bit spell," he said. "I want to change these old clothes of mine into nice ones for the party."

"The only reason I'd lend you a change-a-bit spell is to change you from a lazy, sly old fellow into a hard-working, decent one," said Ma sharply. "If you want new clothes, earn them. Get along now! I'm expecting a visitor, my brother, Mr Rumbustious. He'll soon send you

packing if you're round here when he comes."

Dozey didn't like Mr Rumbustious, so he walked off, annoyed. He went through the woods, muttering to himself.

It was a very hot day, and Dozey soon felt tired. He sat down under a bush and went to sleep. He dreamed a wonderful dream. In his dream he had a marvellous new suit of clothes, from a hat with a feather in, to a blue silk waistcoat and shoes to match.

And would you believe it, when he

awoke, the very first thing he saw hanging on a tree near-by was a fine suit of clothes, with a feathered hat, a shirt, waistcoat, trousers, shoes and coat! Dozey was too astonished for words.

"My word! Look at that! My dream's come true. I'm a lucky fellow today, no doubt about that! Ha! I'll dress myself in these and then go and show myself to old Ma Shuffle!"

So he took off his own things and threw them down. He dressed himself in the smart new suit of clothes and felt very grand indeed.

He strode to the nearby pond and looked at himself in the clear water. "Sir Magnificent Dozey!" he said, and bowed to his own reflection. Then he thought he would go and parade up and down the village street and let everyone see him and admire him.

Off he went, the feather waving in his hat. It was a pity he hadn't washed himself in the pool, and it was a pity too that he hadn't combed his hair that morning!

Everyone stopped and stared at this well-dressed Dozey, as he paraded up and down, nodding and bowing.

"Where did you get those clothes, Mr Dozey?" asked little Button in surprise.

"I dreamed them and they came true!" said Dozey grandly.

"A very useful sort of dream," said Button disbelievingly, and ran off.

After he had shown himself off for half an hour, Dozey went to Ma Shuffle's. Ho, wouldn't she stare! He wondered if her brother Mr Rumbustious was there yet. He didn't like him at all, too noisy and very rude at times to people like Dozey. Well, Dozey was certain that Mr Rumbustious had never in his life been clever enough to dream a dream that immediately came true!

Dozey thought he would peep in at the window of Ma's cottage to see if Rumbustious had arrived yet. So he went round into the garden, and was just about to peep through the window when he heard Mr Rumbustious's enormous voice booming away inside.

"I tell you, Ma, if I get hold of that fellow I'll throw him up to the moon! The thief! The robber! The mean, sneaking fellow!"

"Well, Rumbustious," began Ma's voice, but her brother interrupted again immediately.

"I was walking through the woods, and I was hot. I came to the pool – it looked so

clear and cool. So I pulled my clothes off
– my best ones, mind – and into the pool
I went. And I tell you, Ma, when I came
out my clothes had gone – yes, even my
new feathered hat – and these filthy rags
were left instead. Gr-r-r! If I get hold of
that fellow, I'll throw him up to—"

"Yes. You said that before, Rumbustious," said Ma. "But let's think – who in the world could it have been? Who would dare to do a thing like that? He would have to walk away in your grand clothes and everyone would see him!"

Outside the window Dozey's knees began to knock together. His face went pale. He felt very peculiar indeed.

His dream hadn't come true! Mr Rumbustious had come along while he had been dozing, hadn't seen him and had undressed and gone for a swim – and while he was in the water, he, Dozey, had woken up and dressed in Mr Rumbustious's clothes. Whatever was he to do now?

"I tell you, if I catch that fellow, I'll throw…" began Rumbustious again, in his enormous voice. That was too much for poor Dozey. He ran to the gate, and little Shuffle saw him from the door!

"Ma! There's the thief; Mr Dozey! He's got all Uncle's clothes on!" cried Shuffle, and out he went with Mr Rumbustious to catch Dozey.

Well, Mr Dozey's knees were still knocking together, so he couldn't run very fast, and very soon he was being marched into Ma's kitchen by Shuffle and his uncle.

"I can explain it to Mr Plod the village policeman," said Rumbustious. "And after that I'm going to throw you up to—"

"No, no, no!" cried Dozey in fright. He

turned to Ma Shuffle. "Ma, save me! It was all a mistake! What can I do to show you it was?"

"Oh, well, now you're talking sense," said Ma. "Didn't I tell you this very morning there was some weeding to do, and the path to be swept, and a corner that wants digging – and..."

And that's how it came about that Mr Dozey spent three whole days working hard in Ma Shuffle's garden, with little Shuffle keeping an eye on him through the window. He's not going to the party, though – no, he doesn't like meeting anyone just now. They all said the same thing:

"Hi, Dozey! Any more dreams come true?"

The Battle in the Toyshop

One Christmas-time the toyshop in Windy Street was full of the finest toys in the land. There were great furry teddy bears, long-tailed donkeys, golden-haired dolls that could walk and talk, and marvellous soldiers on horseback. All these wonderful toys sat on the front shelves so that they could easily be seen, and behind them sat the cheaper toys.

The cheap toys were rather sad because they couldn't see who came into the shop to buy things; and of course, as you can guess, the most exciting times in a toy's life are when someone comes into the shop to buy something. Suppose that someone should buy them! All the toys hoped they would soon be bought and have a home of their own.

One night the cheap toys began to complain to the more expensive toys.

"Don't you think you could give us a little more room?" they asked.

"This big teddy bear is sitting down hard on my tail," said a little clockwork mouse.

"And nobody can see us; we're quite hidden!" said a little brown dog, a pink cat, and a blue rabbit.

"A good thing too!" said the biggest bear, rudely. "Who wants to see common little things like you, when beautiful toys

like us are here to be bought?"

"Some people can't afford to buy expensive toys like you," said a cheap wooden Dutch doll. "They want us for their children, and let me tell you this, you conceited bear – I have heard it said that many a child loves a little wooden doll like me better than all the furry bears or donkeys in the toyshop!"

"Pooh!" cried the biggest bear. "I don't believe it! Look at me, Dutch doll – I and my brother bears here are the finest toys in the shop!"

"Excuse me," said the tallest golden-haired doll, in a little high voice, "what nonsense you talk, Bear! We, the dolls, are easily the best toys here. We are the most expensive, anyhow."

"You talk rubbish," the bear said rudely. "Why, only the girls like you dolls – boys *and* girls like us bears. So just be quiet!"

All the dolls stood up in anger to hear the bear talk so rudely to them. The bear didn't care. He and his brothers made rude faces at the dolls.

"Now listen to us!" said all the marvellous toy soldiers together, for they only had one voice between them. "Listen to us! We are the kings of this shop. We have swords and rifles, and we are the most powerful toys here. You dolls and bears don't know what you are talking

about – best toys indeed! *We're* the best!"

Then the donkeys sat up straight and frowned very hard at the cheeky soldiers.

"You silly little things!" said the biggest donkey. "Why, the whole lot of you would go into one of our boxes! You're all talking nonsense, bears, dolls, and soldiers. The donkeys are the best toys of all, and we are the kings of this shop, and the king of every playroom too!"

Well, dear me, you should have heard the dolls screaming, the bears shouting, and the soldiers clanking their swords when the donkey said that. How angry they all were! And then the Great Toy-shop Battle began, a battle that is still talked of in every toyshop in the country.

The dolls rushed at the bears and began to smack them hard, and the bears doubled up their furry paws and began to punch the angry dolls. The soldiers drew their swords and marched on the donkeys, who at once kicked out and began to knock the soldiers down from the shelves to the floor.

Smack, smack! went the dolls.

Punch, punch! went the bears.

Clang, clang! went the soldiers.

Kick, kick! went the donkeys, and the soldiers tumbled one by one off the shelf, and went clattering down to the floor below, where they broke and lay still.

The cheap toys were frightened. They crept right to the back of the shelves and crouched there, quite still. They didn't want to join the fight. They were so afraid of being broken, and a broken toy is never sold, you know.

When the battle ended at last, what a dreadful sight was to be seen! All the dolls had their dresses torn, and three had cracks right across their pretty faces. The bears had bald patches all over them, where the dolls had pulled out handfuls of fur. All the soldiers were broken, except two that had fallen on the carpet – and every single donkey had its mane and tail slashed to ribbons by the swords of the fierce little soldiers.

When the toyshop woman came into her shop the next morning to open up, what a dreadful shock she got! She stared all round and could hardly believe her eyes.

"What's happened in the night?" she said at last. "Why, half a dozen cats from outside must have got in, and had a fight with all the toys. Oh dear, oh dear, what a dreadful thing! All the most expensive toys are spoiled! I shall have to send them to the jumble sale. I can't possibly sell them to my customers here!"

Just at that moment the door opened and in came a fat, jolly-looking man.

"Good morning," he said. "I'm holding a Christmas party today for twenty children, and I want lots of toys. Have you dolls, teddy bears, soldiers, and donkeys?"

"I had," said the toyshop woman, sadly. "But look, something has happened in the night and they're all spoiled."

"What a strange thing!" said the jolly man, in surprise. "But never mind – I see you have lots of nice little toys quite unspoiled. I will take some of those."

Then, to their great delight, the clockwork mouse, the pink cat, the blue rabbit, the brown dog, the wooden doll, the Jack-in-the-box, and many other cheap toys were taken down from the shelves and put on the counter for the man to see.

"Very nice, very nice indeed!" said the jolly man, picking up the pink cat and making it squeak by squeezing it in the middle. "I shall be able to buy far more of these cheap toys than I could buy of the expensive ones, and I daresay the children will be better pleased to have four toys each instead of one!"

He bought eighty little toys and packed them carefully into the big case he had brought. Then he paid for the toys, said goodbye to the woman, and went off, delighted with all the toys he had bought. As for the toys, they were filled with joy too, to think they would soon have homes of their own with children to play with them.

The teddy bears, donkeys, dolls and soldiers were all picked up and popped into a sack for the jumble sale. How sad they were!

"Why did we think such a lot of ourselves?" whispered a doll.

"We're being sent away like rubbish!" said a bear, almost crying with shame.

"Well, it's our punishment for being vain and foolish," said the biggest donkey. "We shall be sold for a few pennies each, and we're not worth any more now. We must just make up our minds to bear it, and be as nice as we can to the children who get us. But, oh, how silly we have been!"

And they certainly had been foolish, hadn't they?

Boastful Brenda
and the Brownies

There was once a little girl called Brenda. She had curly hair, bright blue eyes and a very loud voice.

Nobody liked her very much because she boasted all day long.

"You should see my new doll!" she would say. "It's the finest doll in the world. It can talk and walk, and it has the loveliest dress of blue silk."

Presently she would boast about something else – perhaps the good dinner she had had, or the new dress her mother had made for her.

"Ooh, you should have seen the treacle pudding we had for dinner! I guess it was bigger than any pudding you had! And goodness me, you should see my new dress! My mother made it and it's the best dress in the town!"

Now the other boys and girls didn't like to hear such a lot of boasting. They had nice things too, but as soon as they said anything about them Brenda laughed and said she had something much nicer!

"She's a boaster!" said the other children. "She does nothing but say what wonderful things she has and does. And she doesn't have anything better than we have, really. Why, she had a hole in her sock yesterday, and the new doll she boasted about isn't even as big as Anne's old one. Brenda's a boaster! Boastful Brenda, that's what we'll call her!"

Brenda didn't know the children called her that. She just went on boasting about this, that and the other. And one day something happened.

Brenda was walking home by herself from school one day when she met a strange-looking little man, dressed in brown and red. He was walking down the field-path towards her and they met at the stile. He stood aside for Brenda to get over and up she jumped easily and gracefully.

"You jump well," said the little man, admiringly. That was quite enough to set Brenda boasting, of course.

"Oh, we do gym every day at school," she said, "and we have jumping and running, you know. I'm the best at jumping and the quickest at running. You should see me run!"

Now what Brenda said was not true – she was not the quickest at running, and although she could jump quite well, all the boys could beat her. But she badly wanted the little man to think she was wonderful.

96

"Dear me!" he said, "and what else can you do?"

"Oh, I can sing like a bird," said Brenda, "and you should see the pictures I can draw. The teacher says they are wonderful. My writing is very good too, and as for sums, why, I can beat everybody when I try!"

"Marvellous, marvellous!" said the little red and brown man. "Tell me some more."

Brenda was only too ready to talk about herself. Soon she was telling the stranger all about her wonderful toy car, her extraordinary walking clown, her fine new dress and her silver mug that her uncle had given her last birthday.

"And you should see me at home!" she ended up. "Why my mother and father think I'm so clever and good that they never punish me, but they listen to what I say and take my advice. They think I'm wonderful."

"Well, you're certainly a wonderful boaster," said the little man. "I never heard anything like it. I wish you'd come and see my family. They're the most marvellous boasters I've ever met, but I really believe you would beat them all."

Brenda was offended. She didn't like to be told that she was boasting.

"I don't know what you mean by telling me I'm boasting," she said crossly. "I'm telling you the truth."

"Oh no, you're not," said the red and brown man, laughing. "You may think you are, but really you're only boasting. But you do it very well. I've never met such a good boaster."

Brenda was just going to walk off in a temper when the little man put his hand on her arm.

"Come and see my family," he said. "They are the Boasting Brownies and everyone in Fairyland knows them. Do come. They live quite near."

Well, Brenda was excited when she heard that fairies were nearby. What an adventure to boast about to the other children. Oh, yes, yes she must certainly see these brownies.

"Yes, I'll come and see your family," she said. "But don't tell me I boast, or I'll go straight home, and I run so fast that you couldn't possibly catch me."

"Come along then," said the brownie, and he took Brenda's arm. He led her to a big oak-tree, and pressed a little knob on the trunk. A bell rang inside the tree and then, to Brenda's enormous surprise and delight, a small round door opened in the tree-trunk and she saw a little curling flight of steps going downwards!

"Down we go," said the brownie, and down they went, and down and down. At last the stairs came to an end and Brenda found herself in a passage lit by a swinging lantern. Big tree-roots showed up here and there, so the little girl knew she was far down below the wood.

"This way," said the brownie, and he hurried her along the passage until they came to a small door. The brownie opened it and to Brenda's astonishment she found herself in a very strange new world.

"This is Fairyland," said the brownie, waving his hand round. "It's always nearby, but only a few people know that."

It was a lovely place. There was sunshine everywhere. The trees were small and covered with bright flowers. The fields looked like colourful carpets, they were so well-spread with flowers – brilliant blossoms of blue and yellow that Brenda had never seen before. Little crooked houses stood here and there, and pixie-folk went about their business, their long wings reaching behind them. Some of them flew and some of them walked. Brenda stared as if she were in a dream.

"Oh, won't the other children envy me when they hear about this!" she said.

"I don't believe you can talk without boasting, can you?" asked the brownie, curiously. "I do wonder if you'll beat my family at boasting!"

They went down a winding road and Brenda stared in delight at the people they met. Once the brownie stopped to speak to a sandy rabbit with a red scarf round his neck, and Brenda stared at him so hard that she made him quite nervous.

"Isn't she a starer?" he said in a low voice to the brownie.

"No, she's a boaster," said the little man. "My, can she boast! Would you like to hear her?"

"Oh, no, thank you," said the rabbit in a hurry and hurried off down the road.

"I should have liked to have spoken to him," said Brenda.

"Well, he wouldn't have liked it," said the brownie. "Didn't you see him run off?"

Brenda felt cross, but her temper soon went as she walked on down the road with the brownie, seeing stranger and stranger sights with every step. When she saw a doll walking arm in arm with a teddy-bear she stood and stared in surprise, for although she had a walking doll at home, this doll seemed really alive.

"You mustn't stare like that," said the brownie. "People will think you're a starer instead of a boaster. Look, here is my house. I hope all my family are at home. They will be so pleased to see you!"

Brenda saw a strange little house, perfectly round, with an enormous amount of chimneys sticking out of the top.

"Why has it so many chimneys?" she asked in surprise. "Surely you haven't so many fireplaces in that little house?"

"Oh no, we only have one fireplace," said the brownie. "But my family like to

have a house with more chimneys than any one else. It gives them something to boast about, you see."

"It sounds silly to me," said Brenda.

"Boasting always sounds silly," said the little man, and Brenda couldn't think of anything to say to that. They went up the garden path and the brownie opened the door, calling: "Anyone at home?"

Three brownies, very like Brenda's friend, rushed to the doorway, all talking at once. Brenda put her hands to her ears, for the noise was dreadful. At last the noise stopped and the brownies looked at Brenda in surprise.

"Who's this?" they asked.

"It's Boastful Brenda," said the brownie. "I brought her because I really believe she can beat you all at boasting."

"Oh, she couldn't do that," said the three brownies together. "We're the best boasters in Fairyland. We'll have a match with this little girl and see who is the best!"

"Would you like a chocolate bun?" the first brownie asked Brenda. "We made some this morning. Do sit down and make yourself at home. My name is Binks, and the other three are Tip, Cherry and Buffle. Where are the buns?"

Tip got them from a cupboard and offered one to Brenda. She took it and bit into it.

"Quite a nice bun," she began. "But you should see the ginger buns my

106

mother makes! They're lovely – so nice and hot with the ginger in them."

"Oh, that's nothing," said Buffle, eating a bun quickly. "Why, I once made a ginger cake that was so hot it went off like a gun as soon as it was cut! You should have seen it!"

"I don't believe that," said Brenda.

"What, you don't?" said Buffle. "Well, look here! Here's a ginger cake just like the one I was telling you about."

To Brenda's enormous astonishment the brownie lifted up his hand and took from the empty air a big ginger cake. He set it down on the table and took up a knife.

"Now this cake is just as hot as the one I told you about," he said. "It will go off like a gun when I cut it."

He cut it. *Bang*! It exploded in the air and a bit of ginger cake hit Brenda on the nose.

"There you are," said Buffle proudly. "Do you believe me now?"

"I suppose so," said Brenda. "Do you believe me too?"

"No, I don't," said Buffle.

"Well, it isn't fair," said Brenda crossly. "You can take ginger cakes out of the air and I can't. Anyway, I know how to spell 'rhinoceros' and 'hippopotamus' and I'm sure you don't!"

"Yes, we can then!" said all the brownies at once. "And we know how to spell 'killumfhugtonipomurath' and 'fillumtrimbletigohfunperult' and you don't. Ho ho!"

"I never heard those words in my life," said Brenda. 'I believe you made them up."

"Well, we can spell them and you can't!" said Tip. "You should just see all the marvellous things we can do! Why, Buffle can run like a hare, Cherry can jump right over a gate, and I can walk on my hands for half a mile!"

"I can run well too," said Brenda, finishing her chocolate bun. "I can jump the best in my school, and if you showed me how to walk on my hands I could do it better than you!"

"Come on outside then, and we'll have a race!" cried Buffle. They all went out into the road and stood in line, with Binks to give the signal for starting.

"One, two, three, go!" he cried, and away went the three brownies and Brenda. But, dear me, they ran fifty times as fast as she did, and when the race was over, how they laughed at her!

"Ho, ho! Fancy saying you could run fast! Why you couldn't race a tortoise. You're a terrible slowcoach!" cried Tip. "Look at me walking on my hands, now! Could you do that?"

"Of course I could if I wasn't tired," said Brenda. "Anyway, it's a silly thing to do when you've got feet to walk on."

"Oh, no it isn't," said Tip at once. "Because when your feet are tired, you can walk on your hands. Go on, Brenda, try it."

But Brenda wouldn't because she knew she couldn't.

"Well, jump then," said Cherry. "You said you were a wonderful jumper. What about jumping over the gate by that field there?"

"Nobody could do that," said Brenda. "It's much too high."

"I could. Look!" cried Cherry and over

he went as light as a feather. "Come on,
Brenda, it's quite easy."

Brenda ran at the gate and jumped,
hoping that she too would rise over the
gate as easily as Cherry.

But of course she didn't, and down she
came, flat on her nose. How she howled!

"Cheer up," said Binks kindly. "You
shouldn't have boasted about your
jumping, then Cherry wouldn't have told
you to try to beat him at it. Look, you've
made your nice dress all dirty."

"It doesn't matter," said Brenda,

getting up. "I've got six more dresses at home, all new. I've more dresses than any other girl at school."

"Ah, you haven't as many clothes as we have, though!" said Buffle. "I've got twenty-eight coats, all different!"

"And I've got sixty-two hats, all the same," said Tip.

"And I've got one hundred and two shoes, all for the left foot," said Cherry.

"Don't tell such silly stories," said Brenda.

"Well, come and look then," said Buffle and he dragged the little girl indoors again. He opened a cupboard and sure enough there were twenty-eight coats there, all different! Then in another cupboard Brenda was shown an enormous pile of hats, all exactly the same, and on a long shelf she saw scores of shoes, all for the left foot. The little girl was too surprised to say anything, though she longed to ask why all the shoes were for the same foot.

"You're not much good as a boaster really," said Buffle. "You're not half as good as we are. We'd better give her the Boaster's Beautiful Drink, hadn't we, brothers? That will do her a lot of good."

Now Brenda was thirsty, otherwise she certainly would have refused to take such a strange-sounding drink. But when she saw the lovely fizzy stuff being poured into a glass and smelled the nice orange-smell she thought she must just sip it. The sip tasted so delicious that she drank the whole glassful at once!

"You'll be sorry you did that," said Binks, staring at her.

"Won't she be surprised!" said Buffle. "Oh, we shall be able to boast that we made a little human girl drink our magic Boaster's Beautiful Drink!"

Brenda wished she hadn't drunk it. She decided to go home at once and asked Binks to take her back to the hollow tree. So back they went, and Tip, Buffle and Cherry went with them, boasting so hard all the way that Brenda couldn't get a word in!

It wasn't until the little girl was back at school that afternoon that she found out what the magic drink did! She began to boast about going to Fairyland, of course, and as soon as she spoke, a curious thing happened to her! She felt herself swelling up like a balloon! All the children cried out in surprise.

"Oh, Brenda! What's happening to you? You're blowing up like a balloon!"

Brenda stopped boasting at once, and she grew back to her own size again. She was frightened. Oh, that horrid Boaster's

Beautiful Drink! How dared those brownies give it to her? She sat as still as could be in the seat, doing her writing, and she didn't say another word until the teacher came round to correct what she had done.

"I haven't made a single mistake," she boasted. "And I didn't yesterday, either. I was the only girl who—"

Brenda stopped and looked down at herself. How dreadful! She was blowing up like a balloon again! *Pop*! That was one of her buttons flying off.

"Dear me, Brenda," said the teacher, "you are getting very fat lately. Have you been eating a lot of cream and butter at home?"

"Oh yes," said Brenda at once. "My mother always gives me cream with my porridge, and we have the best butter we can—"

She stopped again, because she was blowing up into a very big balloon-like child this time. All the other children stared with wide-open eyes. The teacher passed on to the next child and said no more. Brenda went very red and took up her pencil to write again. After a while she went down to her own size.

At playtime that afternoon the children crowded round Brenda. They couldn't think what was happening to her.

"You know, Brenda," said one of them, "we think you *must* have been to Fairyland today, because such funny things keep happening to you – and they always happen when you start boasting, don't they?"

"Yes, they do," said Brenda humbly.

"I didn't know I boasted so much. Oh dear, I do hope I don't swell up like a balloon every time I boast."

"You'd be like a balloon all day long!" said a little girl, with a laugh. "You're a dreadful boaster, Brenda!"

And very soon Brenda found out what a terrible boaster she was! She blew up like a balloon twelve times the next day – but after that she began to be more careful! In a week she only began to swell up about twice a day, and after that hardly at all. She had rather a bad time

after her birthday, because she so badly wanted to boast about all the marvellous presents she had – but as soon as she felt herself getting like a balloon she stopped talking at once, and soon went down again.

Now she is quite cured and never boasts at all. She wants to go back and tell those Boasting Brownies that she never boasts now, but she can't find the knob on the trunk of that hollow oak-tree. Isn't it a pity?

Cosy's
Good Turn

Bundle came running into the garden to find Cosy. He had an old and rather smelly kipper in his mouth.

He dropped it and barked for Cosy. "Cosy! Cosy! Now where can that cat be? What on earth's the good of finding this nice old kipper for her, out of Mrs Brown's dustbin, if she doesn't come when she's called?"

Cosy sat on top of the wall, washing her face with her paws. She had heard Bundle barking, but she didn't hurry down to see what he wanted.

"I expect he wants to play chase-my-tail or roll-over-and-over," thought Cosy. "What silly games he knows!"

"Woof, woof!" barked Bundle, and then a faint smell of kipper came to Cosy's

119

nose. She sniffed. Then she leaped straight down from the wall and ran to Bundle, her tail up in the air behind her.

"I thought you were never coming," said Bundle. "I've done you a good turn, Cosy. I've found you an old kipper. It's been eaten a bit, but it smells fine. I was just going to eat it myself if you didn't come at once!"

Cosy purred, and rubbed herself against Bundle's silky coat. "You're kind to do me a good turn," she said.

"Well," said Bundle, watching Cosy eat the kipper, "you know what Mistress always says, don't you? She says, 'One good turn deserves another.'"

"Does she really?" said Cosy. "Well, you do me another good turn, then, Bundle. I don't mind."

"Don't be silly. It doesn't mean that I do you another good turn," said Bundle. "It means that you do me one – in return for mine, you see."

"Oh," said Cosy, crunching up the last of the kipper. "All right. I'll do you a good turn, too. The very next thing you want, tell me and I'll get it for you."

"Thanks very much," said Bundle, pleased.

"I'll let you know when I want something. You do smell nice, Cosy. You smell of kipper now, not cat. Come and lie down beside me so that I can keep on sniffing you."

Now, the very next day was hot, so hot that Bundle lay and panted with his tongue out. Someone had spilled his water and there was none to drink. There were no puddles anywhere. It was too far to go to the stream. But oh, how thirsty he was!

"You look silly with your tongue out like that," said Cosy. "Do put it back."

"It comes out as soon as I put it in," said Bundle. "It always does that when I'm hot. Oh, how thirsty I am! Is there any milk about, Cosy? There's no water."

"I've drunk all mine," said Cosy. "I'll go and see if there's any milk in the larder, Bundle. If there is, I know how to knock the jug over and spill the milk on the floor. Then you can come and lick it up."

But the larder door was shut. It always was when Cosy was anywhere about. She went back to Bundle and lay down.

"The larder door's shut," she said. "You'll just have to be thirsty, Bundle."

"Well, why can't you do me that good turn you promised me?" said Bundle. "I'm very thirsty, and you ought to do something about it. You do me my good turn now. Get me some milk to drink!"

"If I knew where the milk came from I'd go and get some for you," said Cosy. "Where does the milkman get his milk from?"

"From a cow, silly," said Bundle. "All our milk comes from cows."

"Does it really?" said Cosy, in surprise. "Well, I never knew that before! How kind of the cows! I know, Bundle – I'll take a jug and go and ask that big red-and-white cow in the field for some milk for you. That would be an awfully good turn, wouldn't it?"

"Yes," said Bundle, panting. "Hurry up then or I shall die of thirst!"

Cosy got a little jug. Then she set off to the fields. Daisy, the big red-and-white cow, was lying down in a cool corner, chewing.

"Cows are always chewing, they never seem to stop," thought Cosy. "Hello, Daisy! Do you think I could possibly have some milk, please?" she asked.

"Well," said Daisy, still chewing, "one good turn deserves another, you know. There's some lovely dark green grass in the next field, all long and juicy, but I can't reach it over the hedge myself. You go and get me a bit of that and I'll fill your jug for you."

"All right," said Cosy, and she ran to the hedge. She squeezed through it and looked about for the grass. She soon saw it growing by a moist ditch, long and juicy. Clopper the horse was standing near it, munching.

Cosy ran to get the grass. She began pulling it up. Clopper stopped munching and stared straight at her.

"Hey!" he said. "That's my grass. It's the best grass in the whole field."

"Oh," said Cosy. "Well, I want some for Daisy the cow, then she'll give me some milk. Can't I take some?"

"Now look here, one good turn

deserves another," said Clopper. "You can have some of my grass if you'll do something for me."

"I seem to be doing no end of good turns," said Cosy.

"Well, I'm longing for a nice green apple," said Clopper. "See that cottage over there? Well, in the back garden there's an apple-tree, and it's got fine green apples on it. You get me one of those and I'll let you take some of that grass."

"All right," said Cosy, and she ran over the field towards the cottage. She jumped up on the wall round it and then down into the garden. Then in a second she was up the apple-tree.

She bumped her head hard against the biggest green apple she could see. It fell to the ground with a bump. Cosy was just about to run down the tree when she heard a cross voice:

"What are you doing up there, cat, knocking down my apples?"

Down below was a plump little woman, trying to mend a clothes-line so that she could hang out her washing. She was looking up at Cosy, surprised and cross.

"Well, you see, I wanted to get an apple

for Clopper," said Cosy. "Could I have the one I knocked down?"

"Well, one good turn deserves another," said the plump little woman. "If you'll go and borrow Mrs Miggle's rope for me, then I'll give you the apple. My clothes-line is broken and I must have another!"

"Another good turn!" sighed Cosy, and ran down the lane to the next cottage, where Mrs Miggle was sitting in the sun, shelling peas.

"May I borrow your rope, please?" asked Cosy. "You see, if I take it to your next-door neighbour, she will give me an apple for Clopper, and he will give me his best grass for Daisy, and she will give me milk for Bundle. I am trying to do him a good turn."

"So you want my rope!" said Mrs

Miggle. "Well, what I always say is: 'One good turn deserves another.' If I lend you my rope, you must do something for me. You run down to the old man who lives at the corner, and ask him to let me have just a few more peas. I haven't enough. Take this basket with you."

"I keep on and on doing good turns!" said Cosy, but she ran off with the basket in her mouth. She soon came to the cottage at the corner. The old man was indoors, looking into his larder. He seemed rather cross.

"Please," said Cosy, "may I have a few peas? Mrs Miggle hasn't enough."

"I'll go and pick them," said the old man. "I like to do people a good turn. But one good turn deserves another, you know, little cat. You can do me a good turn, while I pick the peas."

"I thought you were going to say that," said poor Cosy.

"Now just have a look in this larder of mine!" said the old man. "Mice have been in it again. One ran away just as I opened the door. You catch me those mice

by the time I come back and I'll give you the peas!"

He went out and Cosy sat down quietly behind the door. She could smell plenty of mice, no doubt about that.

"Well, anyway, at least I shall be doing myself a good turn now, as well as the old man," she thought, "because I rather like catching mice!"

Soon Cosy had caught three mice. The old man came with the basket half full of peas. He was delighted to see what Cosy had done for him.

"You've done me a good turn," he said. "And you've done my cat a good turn too – she's too old to catch mice now. Here are the peas. Remember what I said? 'One good turn deserves another!'"

"Goodbye!" said Cosy, and she left the cottage, taking the peas with her.

She went to Mrs Miggle's and put the basket down. "Here are the peas," she said. "Now may I borrow the rope?"

"Here it is," said Mrs Miggle, and gave it to her. "Thank you. You see what I meant when I said, 'One good turn—'"

But Cosy didn't even stop to listen. She tore off to the plump little woman next door, trailing the rope out behind her like a long snake.

"Well, I thought you were never coming!" said the little woman, quite crossly. "I've been waiting such a time. Now, take your apple and go. And always remember, 'One good—'"

"I know it by heart, thank you," said Cosy quite rudely, and then she ran off with the apple. She came to Clopper and rolled it at his feet.

"What a time you've been," said Clopper. "I had quite given you up. I suppose you've been chattering away to someone. Take what grass you want – and remember, 'One—'"

"I don't want to remember it," said Cosy, crossly dragging up the grass. "I've been doing nothing but good turns for ages and ages. You may have done me one good turn, but I tell you I've done heaps! I can't seem to stop doing them. I—"

"What a lot you've got to say," said Clopper. "Ah – now you've got your mouth full of grass and you won't be able to talk. Good. Now remember, 'One—"

But Cosy had fled through the hedge and was on her way to the shady corner in the field where Daisy the cow still lay, chewing away. The little empty jug lay beside her.

"Here's your grass," said Cosy, and dropped it right down beside Daisy.

"I don't really know if I want it now," said Daisy. "You've been so long."

"Well!" said Cosy, crossly. "Of all the

132

ungrateful, unkind—"

"All right, all right," said the cow hurriedly. "I'll have it. Don't lose your temper. You should always do a good turn cheerfully and quickly."

"Don't talk to me about good turns," said Cosy. "Just you do yours, Daisy, and give me some milk for poor old thirsty Bundle. He must have died of thirst by now, I've been so busy doing good turns for everybody!"

Daisy filled the jug with creamy milk, which looked simply lovely. "Now don't spill it," she said. "And remember—"

But Cosy wasn't going to remember anything but the milk. Thank goodness she had got it at last! She went carefully across the field, through the hedge, and into the garden. She looked about for Bundle. Ah, there he was, in the corner where it was cool. How pleased he would be to see the milk! Cosy trotted over and put the jug down carefully beside him.

"There you are, Bundle!" she said. "Lovely milk for you."

Bundle looked down his nose at it. "What, milk again?" he said. "I don't want any more. Mistress came out some time ago and filled your dish with rice pudding and milk. I ate it all up, and I can tell you the milk was very good! But I'm full up now and I don't want any more. It really makes me feel sick to look at all that milk."

"Well!" cried poor Cosy in a rage, and lost her temper altogether. She picked up the jug and threw it at Bundle. The

milk spilled and went all over his silky coat. He was very angry.

"You horrid little cat! Now look what you've done! There's milk all over my coat. And I thought you wanted to do me a good turn, not a bad one!"

"Well, I've tried," said Cosy and tears trickled down her nose. "I've done ever so many good turns. I'm hot and tired and thirsty. I've been ever so far and got ever so many things for people. And when I come back with my good turn for you, Bundle, you don't want it. I feel very upset. And the milk's upset too, and I do so badly want a drink! You've had all my dinner, too. Why did I ever try to do you a good turn? It's all wasted!"

"You can always do me another one some other time," said Bundle. But that wasn't the right thing to say at all.

"What! Another good turn!" cried Cosy. "No, no, Bundle – you can do all the good turns in future. Do you know, I went to Daisy for some milk, and she sent me to Clopper for some special grass she wanted, and Clopper sent me to an apple-tree for an apple, and the woman there sent me to Mrs Miggle's for a rope, and—"

"Goodness gracious!" said Bundle.

"—and Mrs Miggle sent me to the old man at the corner for some more peas, and he told me to catch his mice!" wept poor Cosy. "And then I had to go back and take the peas to Mrs Miggle, and take the rope to the apple woman, and take the apple to Clopper, and take the grass to Daisy, and bring the milk to you, and—"

"And I'd had some, and you upset the milk in a temper," said Bundle. "Poor Cosy! What a shame! But now I'll do you a good turn, if you like! I'll sit quite still and let you lick all the milk that is dripping off my coat. Think what a nice meal that will be for you."

So Cosy sat and licked all the milk off Bundle's coat, and got a lot of hairs down her throat. Now she is still on the wall again, washing herself – and do you know what she is thinking?

"I wonder whether that was really a good turn that Bundle did me, letting me lick the milk off his coat?" she is saying to herself. "Or have I done *him* a good turn again? I've cleaned his coat for him, haven't I, and saved him from having a bath! Now, who did the good turn then?"

What do you think?

Tell-
Tale!

"Here comes Tell-Tale!" said Jinks. "Hello Tell-Tale! That tongue of yours is ready to say something nasty, I'm sure!"

"My name is Roundy, not Tell-Tale," said the little goblin, crossly. "I'm always telling you that."

"And we're always forgetting," said Gobo. "And we shall go on forgetting till you stop telling tales!"

"I don't tell tales," said Tell-Tale. "I just spread the news. I say – have you heard about Mr Stamp-About? He has quarrelled with his old aunt and he called her Mrs Stick-in-the-Mud. I heard him."

"Tell-tale!" said Jinks at once.

The little goblin ran off angrily and looked about for Mrs Listen-Hard. She loved to hear his tales. He met her just

139

down the street. "Oh, Mrs Listen-Hard," he said, "have you heard the latest about the baker's bread? Well, somebody found a mouse-tail in a loaf! What do you think of that?"

"Shocking!" said Mrs Listen-Hard. "Whatever next will he put into his loaves?"

"And did you hear that Jinny Jinks was rude to her teacher yesterday and had to stand in the corner all the

morning?" said Tell-Tale. "All the Jinks children are cheeky – I'd like to stand each of them in a corner. The way they call out after me when I go by!"

"Dear, dear!" said Mrs Listen-Hard. "Well, some people do bring up their children badly, I'm sure!"

Tell-Tale ran round all day long telling his nasty little tales.

He never said anything nice about anyone, but, as tell-tales do, he picked up all the unpleasant bits of news that he could find, and passed them on.

Nobody could stop him; Jinks wouldn't speak to him for a whole month, but Tell-Tale didn't mind. He just went round saying that Jinks was so afraid of him that he dare not open his mouth when he, Tell-Tale, came by. That made Jinks cross and he gave Tell-Tale a stern scolding when he saw him next.

But even that didn't stop him either. And then there came a day when he told tales to quite the wrong person!

It happened that the Wizard of Ho was coming to stay with his brother, Mr

Kindly, in Tell-Tale's village. Tell-Tale got the news first, and ran round to everyone.

"Have you heard the news about Mr Kindly's brother?" he asked. "It's that horrible Wizard of Ho, you know. He's coming here to stay."

"He's not horrible," said Gobo. "He's stern and very clever – but he's kind too, like his brother."

"Well, I've heard tales about him that prove he's not a bit kind," said Tell-Tale. "Did you know he once turned a dog into a shopping-basket, just because it barked at him, and goes shopping with that basket every day?"

"Rubbish!" said Gobo. "Where do you pick up these extraordinary tales? You must make half of them up!"

"And did you hear that the Wizard wouldn't…" began Tell-Tale again – but Gobo walked off. Tell-Tale stared after him angrily.

"How rude he is! I'll go and find Mrs Listen-Hard and tell her of Gobo's bad behaviour!"

Now, the next week, it happened that Tell-Tale had to walk to the farm to get some butter. On the way back he overtook a small cart, drawn by a donkey. It was driven by a funny old fellow, who sat on top of a pile of boxes and bags. He had on an old green suit, and wore a rather shabby hat with a green feather in it.

He called to Tell-Tale. "Hey, you! Am I right for Apple-Tree Village?"

"Oh, no – you're on the wrong road," said Tell-Tale. "I'm on my way there, so I'll guide you, if you like. It's my own village, so I know the way well."

"Jump up then," said the old fellow, and Tell-Tale leaped up and sat on a box.

"What's Apple-Tree Village like?" asked the old man, clicking to his donkey. "It's a nice little place, I've heard, with kindly people."

"Ah – that's what you've heard," said Tell-Tale. "The people are a strange lot – rude, you know – no manners. Some of them aren't honest, either – or kind."

"Dear, dear!" said the old fellow. "But what about Dame Gentle, and Mr Kindly? Surely they are like their names?"

"Not a bit!" said Tell-Tale, enjoying himself. "Dame Gentle smacked me the other day – that shows how gentle she is! And as for Mr Kindly, nobody really likes him. He only pretends to be kind. And that reminds me – he's got a dreadful

144

brother coming to stay with him, a horrible fellow called the Wizard of Ho."

"Really?" said the old man. "And what's so horrible about the Wizard of Ho?"

"Oh, haven't you heard?" said Tell-Tale. "Well, it's said that he's not honest – he goes round stealing things he wants for his spells, if he can't buy them. He stole a bunch of peacock feathers out of Mrs Hey-Diddle's vase on her mantelpiece, when he went calling one day."

"You don't say so!" said the old man.

"Yes – and he was once turned out of the palace for being rude to the prince himself," said Tell-Tale. "And he turned a dog into a shopping-basket for barking at him. Oh, I tell you, he's a bad fellow, and nobody wants him to come and stay in the village."

"Dear me!' said the old man.

"I can tell you, I shall say a few things to him that he won't like, if I see him," said Tell-Tale. "Nobody else will – they're too feeble for words in our village! I'm the only one that sticks up for my own ideas. I'll send that old wizard packing if he doesn't behave himself."

"Is this the village?" said the old man, as they came to a row of pretty little houses.

"Yes," said Tell-Tale. "There's Mr Kindly's cottage, look. He's in his garden – looking out for someone, I should think."

"Yes – he's looking out for me, I expect," said the old man. "He's my brother. I'm the Wizard of Ho. You've been telling me a lot of tales about myself – most interesting! I had never heard them before."

Tell-Tale stared at him in horror. What – this funny old man was the great Wizard of Ho? Without his cloak, without

his great pointed hat – no wonder he hadn't known him!

"Thank you for guiding me," said the wizard, getting down. "Here's something for your trouble." He reached his hand up into the air – and brought down a parrot! A little parrot, straight out of the air. How extraordinary!

"It can talk like you," said the wizard. "It can tell tales, sometimes true, sometimes not, just like yours. It's exactly the right companion for you."

The parrot flew straight on to Tell-Tale's shoulder and squawked in his ear, making him jump. "You haven't washed behind your ears this morning!" it said. "Dirty goblin!"

The wizard took no more notice of Tell-Tale but went to greet his brother, Mr Kindly. Tell-Tale fled down the street, very scared. Goodness – he might have been turned into a black-beetle or a caterpillar! He ran into his house and slammed the door.

"Don't be noisy," said the parrot on his shoulder. "My word, what an untidy place! Don't you ever sweep the floor?"

"Look here – I'm not having this kind of talk from a parrot!" said Tell-Tale, furiously, and tried to grab it off his shoulder. He got such a jab from its curved beak that he burst out crying.

"Well, what a cry-baby!" said the parrot, in a shocked voice. "Where's

149

your hanky? My, what a dirty one!"

There came a knock at the door, and the milkman put his head in. "Any milk?" he said.

"Oh, milkman, yes – one pint," said Tell-Tale. "I say – did you hear that the baker put a mouse-tail in one of his loaves?"

The parrot gave a squawk. "Milkman, did you know that Tell-Tale doesn't sweep his floor? And I say, have you ever sat on his shoulder and looked behind his ears? He doesn't wash properly! And he's an awful cry-baby. Just now—"

"*Will* you stop it!" cried Tell-Tale, in a rage. "What do you mean saying all those things about me? I won't have it!"

The parrot nibbled his ear, and Tell-Tale yelled and tried to push him off. "No use," said the parrot. "The wizard gave me to you, and here I stay. I'm a chatterbox, I am – just like you!"

What a truly dreadful time Tell-Tale had the next few days. He simply could not get rid of that parrot. It clung to his shoulder wherever he went – and it said the most dreadful things!

As soon as Tell-Tale told a tale about anyone the parrot at once told a few about the goblin. "Listen to me, listen to me!" it would squawk. "Have you heard that Tell-Tale picks apples out of Dame Flap's garden at night? And did you know that he borrowed Flip's barrow and never took it back? It's in his shed. Squaawk!"

"Oh, you fibber!" cried Tell-Tale.

"Who's a fibber?" said the parrot raising the feathers on its head angrily. "You are! Who said the Wizard of Ho

turned a dog into a shopping-basket? You did. You're a fibber!"

"Will you be quiet?" shouted Tell-Tale.

"No," said the parrot. "I'm fond of talking, like you. I'm fond of spreading tales. You can't blame me for that! You're fond of it too. Oh, I say, do you remember the time when you took the sweets away from Mother Jolly's little girl? And shall I tell you about the time when…"

Tell-Tale had to run back home and slam his door then. He just never knew what that parrot would say next. But he couldn't get rid of it. It sat on his shoulder day and night, and he dared not try to push if off because it pecked him so hard with its curved beak.

"You deafen me with your squawks!" complained Tell-Tale. "I hate you! And how dare you tell all those wicked stories about me? They're not true!"

"Half of them are," said the parrot, jigging up and down on Tell-Tale's shoulder in a most aggravating manner. "Some of them aren't. But lots of the tales you tell aren't true either. You stop

telling untruths and I will. See?"

"All right," said Tell-Tale, who was really getting most alarmed at the stories the parrot told about him. Why, if they came to the ears of the village policeman, he might quite well believe them, and pop Tell-Tale into prison!

So Tell-Tale was very careful after that. He didn't tell any untrue tales – but he told plenty of true ones that were not very nice!

"Did you know that Mr and Mrs Binks had a dreadful quarrel yesterday?" he said. "Did you hear that little Pinkity had to write out a hundred lines after school this morning – *I must not be rude to teacher*. Did you know that—"

"My turn, my turn!" shouted the parrot. "Did you know that Tell-Tale hasn't got a toothbrush, so he never cleans his teeth? Did you hear that he wouldn't pay old Mrs Needle what she asked him for making his new suit? Did you know that he never makes his bed, the dirty fellow? Did you—"

Tell-Tale was always going red in the face, always feeling ashamed, always running back home to stop the parrot saying any more. How he hated that bird! But he couldn't get rid of it, no matter what he did.

So one day he went to Mr Kindly's cottage, and asked to see the wizard. Mr Kindly took him into his little front room, where the wizard was reading a book on spells. Tell-Tale knelt down humbly.

"I have come to beg your pardon," he said. "Forgive me for all I said. And I do beg of you to take this parrot away – he is making my life miserable."

"He is only doing what you have often done," said the wizard. "You have made many lives miserable with your tales.

154

Why shouldn't you be made miserable
too?"

"I'll never make people miserable
again," said Tell-Tale. "Please take this
hateful bird away."

"Sir Wizard, did you know that Tell-
Tale always..." began the bird. Tell-Tale
began to cry.

"There you are, you see – he tells tales

about me all the time. Take him away!"

"I can't," said the wizard, gravely. "He'll be with you always now. I made him out of your own nature, you know. He's part of you now. He'll never go away! You're a tell-tale fellow, and he's a tell-tale bird!"

Mr Kindly was sorry for poor Tell-Tale. He patted him on the shoulder. "There's quite an easy way out," he said. "Turn over a new leaf, Tell-Tale. Make yourself kind and truthful – don't run about telling tales and making mischief – and this bird will copy you and be the same!"

"It isn't an easy way out!" wept Tell-Tale. "It's the hardest thing in the world to change myself – you know that."

The little goblin went off, and the tell-tale parrot screeched in delight. "Did you know he went and fell on his knees before the Wizard of Ho? Did you hear that?"

Well – that was a whole year ago now, and I expect you'd like to know what happened. Somebody went to Apple-Tree Village the other day and wanted to

know where Tell-Tale lived.

"Tell-Tale? Who's he?" said Gobo. "Oh, you mean Roundy – the nice little fellow who's got a talking parrot? We don't call him Tell-Tale any more you know. Everyone likes him now – and as for the parrot, well it's a real pet!"

So now we know what happened! Good for you, Tell-Tale – oh, no – I mean Roundy!

A Tale of Two Cowards

"That was a jolly good game," said Bill as he came into the cloakroom to change out of his football things.

"It was," said Jim. "Gracious – look at the bruises I've got today!"

He showed them to the others. His legs were black and blue. He was a courageous little player and never minded tackling anyone, or falling down with a bang.

"You'll be playing for Scotland one day, Jim MacTavish!" said the games master, coming in. "I don't believe you're afraid of anything."

"But Robbie won't be playing for England," said someone, jeeringly. Everyone turned to look at the boy over in the corner. He was pulling his football jersey over his head, and he was glad his face was hidden.

"He's afraid of falling down, aren't you, Robbie?" said Bill. "He gives up the ball at once if he thinks he's going to be bumped over. Baby Robbie!"

"Shut up!" said Robbie. But that didn't stop the boys. Robbie wasn't brave. He tried to be, but somehow he just couldn't. He hated falling over, he couldn't bear a fight, and he was terrified of being punished by anyone.

"I'd hate Robbie to be on my side," said Jim. "He might just as well be

playing for the other side, for all the good he is. He never tackles anyone. He's afraid of getting hurt."

"He'll cry in a minute," said Bill.

It really looked as if poor Robbie was about to cry. The games master looked at him in disgust. "For goodness sake, Robbie, do be your age! I wish I could put a little courage into you. You run fast, and you're good with your feet – you'd be a very fine player if you'd only got more spirit."

Robbie knew that. His father was always telling him that too. But how did you get courage if you didn't seem to be born with any? He looked at Jim with all his bruises. Jim was full of pluck and courage. Jim saw him looking and he grinned.

"Well, baby," he said, "want me to take you home in case someone runs off with you?"

Robbie turned away and began to hunt for his school jersey. All the boys wore navy blue jerseys in class, with the school badge embroidered neatly on

the left. Where on earth was his?

"Someone's taken my jersey, sir," he said at last, when Mr Locke, the games master, shouted at him to be quick. "I can't find it anywhere."

"Who's taken it?" said Mr Locke sharply, looking round at the waiting boys. "You know what I said last week – this hiding of other people's things has got to stop. Whoever has got the jersey must produce it *at once*."

Nobody moved. Each boy looked round

at the next. Who had hidden Robbie's jersey?

The master was angry. "I warn you, if that jersey is not produced now, this very minute, I shall punish the boy very severely when I discover who it is. It will mean staying in from games for a fortnight."

Still nobody said anything.

"Very well," said Mr Locke. "Put your overcoat on instead of your lost jersey, Robbie and come into the class like that. Somebody is being extremely foolish."

The boys giggled as they saw poor Robbie putting on his overcoat. He felt silly, having to go into class like that but it was a very cold day and he couldn't sit in his shirt! The games master saw them into the classroom and then went back to the cloakroom. He hunted for the lost jersey in every likely corner, but it was nowhere to be found. What in the world had happened to it? No boy had had any chance of hiding it anywhere but in the cloakroom.

He went off, still feeling angry.

He disliked being disobeyed. When he found out who the culprit was he would soon show him that it didn't pay to be disobedient!

Robbie was upset about his missing jersey. Now his mother would be angry with him. He would probably have to empty his money-box and give her the money for a new one – and it really wasn't his fault at all. If only he needn't tell her! He hated being grumbled at.

"In fact, I'm just a coward," thought Robbie in despair. "I'm afraid of everything – afraid of being hurt, afraid of being punished, afraid of being grumbled at. I wish I had a friend who was strong and brave and who would help me – someone like Jim. But the plucky boys laugh at me. Not one of them would be friends with somebody like me."

He didn't find his jersey, and his mother was angry with him. As he thought, he had to take money from his money-box to help buy a new one. He wondered where his jersey was. Had somebody hidden it?

Jim wondered where it was too. He saw Robbie as he went home, and called out after him: "Well, Robbie, scared of telling your mother about your jersey? Don't cry too much, will you?"

He told his own mother about Robbie, as he sat eating his tea. "He's an awful baby," he said, scornfully. "He just lets anyone take the ball away from him at games, Mum. And he's so scared of falling down that he'll never even bump

into any of us to get the ball away. Now he's lost his silly jersey, and I bet he's howling this very minute because his mother is cross with him."

"You're always so down on poor Robbie," said his mother. "Strong people like you should help the weak, you know, Jim, not make them weaker still by jeering at them. That's one thing I don't like about you. Poor old Robbie. I think it was unkind to hide his jersey."

"Pooh!" said Jim, rudely – but he said it under his breath, so that his mother wouldn't hear. He got up from his tea.

"I'm awfully hot," he said. "I can't think why. I'll go upstairs and take off this thick jersey and put a thinner one on."

He went upstairs two at a time. He pulled his jersey off over his head and tossed it on the bed – and then he stared down at himself in great astonishment. He still had a jersey on! He looked at the one on the bed – and then at the one he had on, puzzled.

"Why, what's happened?" he said – and then of course, he knew! He had put on his own jersey, when he had changed after games – and without thinking what he was doing, he had picked up someone

else's jersey and put that on too! He had worn two jerseys – no wonder he felt hot.

"My word, the second one must be Robbie's," he thought. He picked it up and looked at the name sewn into the collar. "Yes – Robert Simpson – gosh, so that's where his jersey went. Nobody hid it; I put it on over mine by mistake."

He sat and thought for a moment. This wasn't very nice. He'd jeered at Robbie about his jersey and all the time he, Jim, had got it on. It was really very awkward. Now the boys would jeer at him, and what would Robbie say? He would certainly pay back Jim for all his jeers and sneers.

Then there was the games master. Would he believe Jim when he told him that he had worn Robbie's jersey by mistake? Would he believe that any boy would be silly enough to put on two jerseys and not notice it? What about that punishment he had threatened? No games for a fortnight for the boy who had taken the jersey – and there was a school match on next week.

Jim was full of dismay. He glared at Robbie's jersey and shook his fist at it. It was going to be the cause of a very great deal of trouble. Then another thought struck Jim. Need it be the case of any trouble? Nobody knew Jim had the jersey. Nobody had noticed that he had put on two. Well, then, if he said nothing about it all, but just pushed it into somebody's locker where it would sooner or later be found, nobody would ever know how it got there. He wouldn't be laughed at, Robbie wouldn't shout at him, and the games master wouldn't stop him playing games for a fortnight.

"Easy!" thought Jim, though he felt very uncomfortable about it. Still, it was a fine way out of trouble. He got up and stuffed the jersey into a drawer. He'd take it to school the next day and push it into an empty locker. It was a very good idea!

But all Jim's plans came to nothing. It happened that his mother came up just then to put some of Jim's clothes away and the very first drawer she opened was

the one into which Jim had pushed
Robbie's jersey. She pulled it out in
surprise and looked at Jim. He was
sitting on the bed, still wearing his own
blue jersey.

"Why, Jim – what's this?" she said,
and she looked at the name on the collar.
"Oh, Jim, it's Robbie's jersey – you told
me he'd lost it. How did it get here? Tell
me the truth, please."

Jim hesitated. He didn't want to tell
his mother at all. She wouldn't think

much of him, he knew. She saw him going red and she was shocked. "Jim, you took the jersey and you got Robbie into trouble. What a cowardly thing to do."

"I didn't take it," said Jim. "Well – at least, I did – but, you see, it was by mistake." He told his mother about the mistake and she listened gravely.

"I see that it was a mistake," she said. "But what horrifies me is that you didn't rush round to Robbie's and own up – you hid it away in a drawer. You meant to say nothing at all about it, Jim. I can see it in your face. Why, you're a coward! You're an even bigger coward than Robbie. You were running away from trouble and leaving somebody else to bear the blame."

Jim couldn't say a word. He suddenly saw how right his mother was. He had been jeering at Robbie for being afraid of things and now here he was, just as much afraid – afraid of owning up and taking whatever punishment there might be in store. He was a coward, too.

He didn't like it. He stared at his mother, very red in the face. She looked back at him sternly. "Well?" she said. "What are you going to do? It's always possible to stop being a coward, you know."

Jim got up. "Yes – I know," he said. "Sorry, Mum. I feel awful. I'm going straight round to Robbie's."

"You're a good boy, really," said his mother, and she looked very pleased. She gave him a sudden hug. "Things seem difficult sometimes, Jim, don't they – but there's only one thing to do, and that's face up to them."

"I'll always do that," said Jim. "Don't worry, Mum. This won't happen again."

He went out with the jersey and was soon knocking at Robbie's door. Robbie opened it. He was very surprised to see Jim.

"Can I come in?" said Jim. "I've got something to say." Robbie took him up to his bedroom in surprise. Why was Jim so solemn?

"Er – Robbie – here's your jersey," said Jim, holding it out to him. "Hope you didn't get into trouble about it. I had it."

"You had it?" said Robbie in amazement. "But why didn't you own up then? You know what Mr Locke said about not having games for a fortnight if you didn't."

"I didn't own up because I didn't know I had it," said Jim. "I put my own jersey on, and then by mistake I put yours over it but I didn't know I had. Now go on – jeer at me – go and blab to the master. Laugh at me for a fortnight for having to stay in and work when you're all playing games. I deserve it."

Robbie stared at him in surprise. "You put on two jerseys!" he said. "Two! Oh gosh – how frightfully funny! Didn't you feel hot and fat? I thought you looked fat in class, you know!"

And then, to Jim's amazement Robbie began to laugh. He laughed and he laughed and soon Jim began to laugh too. Robbie had such a chuckle of a laugh, you couldn't help joining in!

"We don't say a word to the master about all this," said Robbie at last. "Then you won't have to stop playing games. You're so good at them. We simply must have you in the school match next week."

Jim looked in amazement at Robbie. "But I was so mean to you," he said. "Don't you want to get back at me for jeering at you – and getting you into trouble over your jersey?"

Robbie considered. "No – I may be a coward," he said, "but I don't think I'm mean. I want you to play in the match, of course, for the school's sake. And after all, it really was an accident!"

Jim was even more astonished. He turned away and spoke gruffly.

"Look here – what will you think of me when I tell you I wasn't going to give you back your jersey *or* own up – I was going to stuff it into a locker, then nobody would ever have known. My mother found it and she told me I was even more of a coward than you, not to own up!"

Robbie thumped Jim on the back. "Jim, do you mean to say you can be a coward too? That's wonderful! I thought a boy like you never, never could. Well, there's hope for me, then."

Jim turned round. He began to laugh. He simply couldn't help it. It was so funny to be thumped on the back because he had been a coward. He held out his hand to Robbie.

"Come on, shake," he said. "We're
friends from now on, and just remember
this – if you want to stop being a coward,
you can. And I'm jolly well going to see
to it!"

Both boys went to bed that night
feeling surprised and happy. In the
morning Jim went to own up to the
games master, and get his punishment.

But to his surprise Mr Locke laughed.

"Oh, I've already heard about your silly mistake," he said. "Robbie came along and told me. He doesn't want you punished, of course. He's a decent fellow you know, old Robbie."

"I know," said Jim, and went off, delighted. He would play in the match after all!

He told his mother the whole thing. "There you are," she said. "Face up to trouble and see what happens."

The biggest thing that happened, of course, was that the two boys were friends – and you'll want to know if Robbie is still a coward.

Well, he's always one of the boys chosen to play in every school match now, so it's easy to guess the answer!

Father Time and His Pattern Book

One New Year's Eve, in the middle of the night, Robin woke with a jump. He sat up in bed and listened. Whatever could have wakened him?

Then he heard slow footsteps outside his window, and he wondered who it could be wandering around in the garden in the middle of the night!

"Perhaps it is someone who is lost in the snow," he thought. So he jumped out of bed and went to the window. He opened it and leaned out. It was dark outside but he could just make out something moving below.

"Who's there?" he called, and a most surprising answer came up to him:

"I'm Old Father Time! I've come to collect this year's patterns."

"This year's patterns! Whatever do you mean?" said Robin in astonishment. "And what are you doing in our garden?"

"Well, I came to collect your pattern too," said the old man.

"I haven't got a pattern!" said Robin. "You must be dreaming."

"Maybe I am," said Father Time. "But my dreams are true ones. It's cold out here, little boy. Let me in and I will show you some of my patterns."

"I think the dining-room should still be warm," said Robin, excited. "I'll let you in, and we can go into the dining-room for a bit. Shall I wake Mummy?"

"Oh no," said Father Time. "Don't wake anyone. Hurry up and let me in."

Robin slipped downstairs. He opened the front door quietly and someone came in. Robin went to the dining-room and switched on the light. Then he saw his visitor for the first time.

Father Time was an old, old man. His beard almost reached the ground. He had a wise and kindly face, with dreamy, happy eyes and a sad mouth. He carried a great scythe with him, which Robin was most surprised to see.

"What's that for?" he asked. "Did you get it out of our garden shed? It's what we use to cut the long grass."

"This scythe is mine," said Father Time. "I use it to cut away the years from one another. I cut time with it."

"How strange!" said Robin, feeling excited. "Now, do show me the patterns you spoke about! Where are they? And what are they?"

Father Time didn't have any book of patterns. Robin had thought he would have one rather like the book of patterns that mother sometimes got from the man who sold curtains. But except for his scythe he had nothing at all.

"My patterns?" he said. "Oh, I have them all, though you can't see them just at the moment. Everyone makes a pattern of his life, you know. Your brother does. Your friends do. I'll show you any pattern you like to ask me for."

"Well – I'd like to see what pattern my brother made last year," said Robin.

Father Time put down his scythe carefully. He put out the light. Then he held up his hands in the darkness and from the fingers of Old Father Time there flowed a shining ribbon, broad and

quivering as if it were alive. It was as wide as the table, and it flowed down on to it like a cloth, spreading itself flat for Robin to see.

"I say! It's a lovely pattern," said Robin. "I shouldn't have thought my little brother could have made such a beauty. How did he make it?"

"The pattern is made of the stuff he put into each day," said Father Time. "The happy moments – the times he ran to do a kindness – the times he cried with fear or pain. They are all in the pattern. This line of silver is a line of love – he loves very much for it is a beautiful line. This glowing thread shows his happy times – he is a happy little boy. This shimmering piece is a great kindness he did, about the middle of the year. It shines because it shines in everyone's memory."

"Yes, I remember that," said Robin. "I hurt my leg and couldn't go to a party. So Lenny wouldn't go either and he brought me every single one of his toys and gave me them for my own, because he was so sorry for me – even his best railway train that he loves. I shall never forget how kind he was to me. But what is this ugly little line of black dots that keeps showing in the pattern?"

"Those spots come into a pattern when the maker of the pattern loses his temper," said Father Time. "He must be careful, or as the years go on the spots will get bigger and bigger and spoil his pattern altogether."

"Oh dear, I'll have to warn him," said Robin. "Now show me Harry's pattern,

Father Time. You know – Harry Jones. He lives next door. Have you got his for last year?"

"Yes, I collected it tonight," said Father Time. The pattern he had been showing Robin faded away into the darkness, and from Father Time's fingers flowed another one that spread itself on the table as the others had done. It was an ugly pattern, with two or three bright threads lighting it up. Robin looked at it.

"It's not a very beautiful pattern, is it?" he asked.

"No. Harry cannot have done very well with his three hundred and sixty-five days last year," said Father Time sadly. "See – that horrid mess there means greediness and selfishness – and here it is again – and again – spoiling the pattern that the bright threads are trying to make."

"Yes, Harry is selfish," said Robin. "He's an only child, and thinks everything must be for him. What are the bright threads, Father Time?"

Father Time looked at them closely. "They are fine strong bits of pattern," he said. "They are hard work that Harry has done. He is a good worker, and if he goes on trying hard, those bright threads will be so strong that they will run right through those messy bits. Maybe one day he will make a better pattern."

The pattern faded. Robin thought for a moment, and then he asked for another. "Show me Elsa's, please," he said. "She's such a nice girl. I like her."

Once again a pattern flowed over the table. It was a brilliant one, beautiful and even. It would have been perfect except that it seemed to be torn here and there.

"It's lovely except for those torn bits," said Robin.

"Yes – Elsa must be a happy and clever girl," said Father Times. "But alas – look at these places where the pattern is quite spoiled! That means cruelty, Robin – a thing that tears the pattern of our lives to bits. Poor Elsa! She must be careful, or one day her pattern will be torn to pieces, and all her happiness will go."

"How strange, Father Time!" said Robin, astonished. "That's one thing I can't stand about Elsa – she is so unkind to animals. I've often seen her throw stones at them. And yet she's so nice in every other way."

"Tell her about her pattern," said Father Time. "For maybe one day a moment of cruelty will spoil a whole year and more."

"Now show me Leslie's pattern," said

Robin. "He's such a funny little boy, Father Time – so shy and timid, like a mouse! I'd love to see the kind of pattern that he has made this last year."

Once again a pattern flowed in the darkness – but what a strange one! It could hardly be seen. There was no brightness in it, no real pattern to see. It was just a smudge of dingy colours.

"Poor little boy!" said Father Time. "He is afraid of everything! He has put no brightness into his pattern, no happy moments, no kindness – only shyness and fear. Robin, you must help him to

make a better pattern next year. Tell him to have courage and not to be afraid of doing kindness to anyone. Then his pattern will glow and shine."

The pattern faded. Father Time went to switch on the light. "I must go," he said. "I have many other patterns to collect tonight and put into my book of history."

"Wait a minute!" said Robin. "Please, Father Time – may I see my own pattern?"

"Yes, you may," said Father Time. He didn't put on the light, but held up his strange fingers once again. And from them flowed the pattern of all the days of the last year – the pattern made by Robin himself.

Robin looked at it, half fearful, half excited, wondering what he would see. He saw a brilliant pattern, full of bright colours that danced and shone. In it were pools of silvery light, but here and there were smudges of grey that spoiled the lovely pattern he had made.

"Ah, Robin, you have done well this

year to make such a fine pattern," said Father Time, pleased. "You have been happy, for see how the pattern glows. You have worked hard, for see how strong the pattern is, unbroken and steady. You have been kind, for here are the silver pools that shine in the pattern and shine in your friends' memories, too."

"But, Father Time – what are those grey smudges that spoil the pattern here and there?" asked Robin, puzzled. "I don't like them."

"Neither do I," said Father Time. "They show where you spoiled your days by telling untruths, Robin. Truth always shines out in a pattern, but untruths smudge it with grey. See – you did not tell the truth there – and there – and there – and look, as the pattern reaches the end of the year, the grey smudges got worse. You have let that bad habit grow on you and spoil the lovely pattern you were making."

"Yes," said Robin, ashamed. "I have been getting worse about telling

190

untruths, I know. Mummy keeps telling me that. I didn't know they would spoil the pattern of my year, though. I'll be very, very careful next year – I shan't tell a single untruth, then my pattern will be really lovely."

"Be careful nothing else creeps in to spoil it," said Father Time. "I will come next year and show you the pattern you have made. Now, goodbye – I must go. I feel much warmer and I have enjoyed our talk!"

"So have I! It was wonderful," said Robin. "Thank you very much, Father Time!"

The old man slipped out of the house and Robin went back to bed. He dreamed all night long of the year's patterns, and when he woke in the morning he couldn't think whether it had all been a dream or not.

"Anyway, I shall know next New Year's Eve," said Robin. "I shall look out for the old man again then – and see the pattern I have made. I do hope it's beautiful."

Would you like to see the one you made last year? What do you think it would be like? I would love to know.